The Bent Hostage

Even in Central America you can insure against the kidnapping of senior executives. The premiums are high, and awkward questions have to be answered. But if you can spare an executive, the rewards are huge.

Herb Lopwitz, corporate lawyer of Sanitex Inc., can spare any number of executives. In particular, losing John Clark III, son of the chairman, has a certain rightness to it. Engineer a kidnap in the Dominican Republic, and bingo! $25,000. No problem – once the contributions of comically named revolutionary movements, venal police chiefs, hard–as–nails anchorwomen, straight–as–a–die insurance men and confused terrorism experts have been taken into account . . .

The Bent Hostage

The Bent Hostage

Martin Charles

BLOOMSBURY

First published in Great Britain 1991

Copyright © 1991 by Martin Charles

This paperback edition published 1991

The moral right of the author has been asserted

Bloomsbury Publishing Limited, 2 Soho Square, London W1V 5DE

A CIP catalogue record for this book
is available from the British Library

ISBN 0 7475 1016 4

Typeset by Rowland Phototypesetting Limited,
Bury St Edmunds, Suffolk
Printed in Great Britain by
Cox and Wyman Limited, Reading, Berks.

The Bent Hostage

John Clark III was waking up. Blinding sunrays filtered through the window shades. It was no use even to attempt sitting up, so he just lay there drifting. All his memories were blurred to the point of not being memories at all but images, interposed one over the other.

His last vague recollection was waking up and being carried out of the room by a man and yes, that woman. He had been talking with her in the parking lot, when the sudden cold sensation of a gun muzzle in his back had forced him into a van. One of the three hooded men peeled off his jacket, rolled up his shirtsleeve and shoved a hypodermic into his arm. But where was he now? . . . He had been carried out of the room, sat on a hard stool, a paper or something shoved between his hands. A camera flashed once or twice. They had carried him back in and shot him up again. It had hurt that time. This man, this bearded man, could not find his vein easily.

Gradually he became more aware of the rest of his body. As his barely awake mind continued to struggle, he realized how weak he felt. His stomach was empty. His extremities were numb, very numb. His eyes began to focus a little more now. The furniture, the window, the walls began standing still. A certain order threaded through the world around him. He had not eaten since those scrambled eggs, how long ago? As long ago as he could remember.

Just as he started to focus on the objects around him, the foot of the bed, night table, chest, window, the door opened. It was a woman, dressed in fatigues, a full cartridge belt emphasizing the wide curves of her hips. It was not the same woman that Clark remembered from before. Her smile was stunning. 'Hello, I'm Nora,' she said. 'I'm here to take care of you.'

1

'So there it is, gentlemen, in black and white, or should I say red and white.'

The Chairman and President of the Sanitex Equipment Company, New York, slammed the corporate report down hard on the conference table. A large, jowly man, Howard Grover had remained standing during most of his grim oration that morning. He now stared down the curved oak table at each of his Executive Vice Presidents. They had seen him angry on frequent occasions, but never this bad. Some of them looked almost catatonic. Others stared upwards, downwards, sideways, just anywhere to avoid the Chairman's lunging eyes and their own helpless expressions. Only Herbert Lopwitz, the rotund, somewhat cherubic Corporate General Counsel, seemed anything near relaxed. He sat in the leather chair, to the Chairman's right as always, attired in one of his antiquated gray waistcoated suits and puffing at his pipe. Only he could count on remaining secure – as long as Sanitex Equipment remained in existence.

The company's failing performance was not his responsibility. Quite the contrary. It was his deft manipulation of the company's assets, use of personal contacts and well-oiled machinery of bribes and kickbacks which had kept Sanitex Equipment afloat during the last three years. In that time costs had exceeded income by up to twenty million dollars a year.

Much of it was the Chairman's own fault. Although Lopwitz never cared to offend him, he thought Grover was an inflexible, short-sighted and unimagi-

1

native blowhard. He tended towards rejection of most new ideas on how to improve the company's ageing production management and marketing techniques. It had even been a struggle to get his approval for funding to computerize office systems and distribution outlets. But Lopwitz invariably knew the exact moment to capitalize on the Chairman's wrath and recommend yet another chop in personnel. Grover was often reluctant to do this, since a sentimental attachment to old and loyal employees reflected the good side of his nature. Still, the axe that Lopwitz wielded had already cut three members from the board of management, which met this morning. The survivors felt towards the General Counsel like suspected heretics towards the Grand Inquisitor. All of them, that is, except possibly for John Clark III, grandson of the founder, who as head of international sales should otherwise be the most vulnerable. Yet even Clark clearly felt uncomfortable with what Grover was going on to say.

'Our domestic market has not expanded in over two years and we have suffered net losses in our international market. We are out of Europe altogether, barely keeping alive in Canada, lost seven out of eight bids we entered for our equipment in the Middle East – as opposed to three orders we managed to get there last year. We are non-existent in the Far East except for Guam and the Philippines and that's due to our defense contracts. Latin America is the only area where we have not shown a net loss this year, managing to break into a new country with our garbage incineration plant for Ecuador. But even there, we lost one bid for sanitation trucks to West Germans in Venezuela and another to a Spanish company in Argentina. I've abandoned any idea of going into Africa. If we can't compete against the Europeans in our own backyard, going up against them there would be like pissing in the wind!'

John Clark III was tall, lean and handsomely attired in all of his Brooks Brothers paraphernalia. He had been moved from Vice President for finance three months ago, to replace the head of international sales when the garbage trucks for Venezuela had fallen through. But only a month ago Clark had lost the Argentine sale.

The Spanish and Argentines do after all share a common language, John Clark III remembered consoling himself when he got the sad call from Eddie Hernandez, the Cuban American Director for Latin America out of their Miami office. Why he had been put in international sales frankly baffled Clark. He had no international experience to speak of outside of vacations in the Bahamas and the South of France, and did not even have a fluent foreign language. Was it just a stopgap measure to fill the space with a trustworthy member of the Clark family until they found someone else, or some machiavellian machination by Lopwitz?

He had never got on well with the General Counsel and did not elicit much respect from Grover. Clark had joined his family's company just two years ago when just turned thirty-three. He had failed to make it as a broker on Wall Street. His father had already retired as Chief Executive Officer, but retained control of forty percent of the company's stock, matching Grover's share, the rest being divided between Lopwitz's ten percent, his mother's five percent and his own five percent. He had steadily come to the realization that he was not cut out for business, but held back from resigning. His private income was not really enough to keep him afloat in Manhattan, especially with the demands of the glamorous model he had married, who was already turning cold on him and, rumor had it, having an affair. He needed the salary. He also wanted to continue to feel welcome at his father's estate in Middleburg, Virginia, where he could ride to hounds with the finest families in America and get to parties which resembled the beginning of *Gone with the Wind*.

Grover's tone had changed to an urgent pleading. 'Now, gentlemen, I'm not issuing any false threats or trying to scare or alarm you. It's very simple. This company cannot remain solvent for much longer at the rate we are going. Two years ago we were seven million dollars in the red. Last year we went over ten and this year it's almost doubled to twenty. I seriously doubt we can get any of our banks to finance our current deficit unless our sales pick up in the next quarter.' His voice became solemn. 'Otherwise we could face bankruptcy by the end of the year.'

Lopwitz puffed his pipe a bit more frantically now. Grover was admitting the truth. The head of finance, Mr Rowntree, had received a noticeably cool reception at Number 1 Chase Manhattan Plaza when he went to sound out possibilities for a new loan last week. But to attempt a major sales breakthrough in the next few months as Grover was now suggesting amounted to nothing more than a last-ditch effort. Lopwitz did not believe in last-ditch efforts.

'Gentlemen, what we gotta do is pull in our resources and concentrate on areas where we have some certainty of gaining fast ground.' Grover was trying to sound like the master strategist. 'Domestically, this means going after expanding communities in the sunbelt states. Internationally, it means going after the Latin American market. It's there, I believe, that we stand the best chance of improving performance. Clark, I want you to plan a trip through Central America and the Caribbean next month. Take Hernandez from our Miami office . . .'

'But isn't it rather dangerous down there right now, Mr Chairman?' John Clark III was presenting the first challenge to Grover all morning.

'That's exactly why the hell we are going down

4

there, Mr Clark.' Grover enjoyed pulling rank on the son of his former boss. 'It's because there is political instability that our government is putting together a new aid package for the region. The Caribbean Basin Initiative, haven't you been reading the papers? Uncle Sam is going to be pouring lots of foreign aid money into the region to help eradicate poverty and other root causes of the Communist movements that threaten to create new Cubas on our doorstep.'

Grover had obviously just read the White House message to the Organization of American States, Lopwitz was thinking to himself, Sanitex Equipment is going bankrupt and the Chairman of the Board is giving a New Frontier speech.

'Economic aid always includes programs for sanitation and hygiene and, gentlemen, we are going to get a piece of that action.'

Grover was dreaming, the only thing coming out of Washington was a lot of talk. It would be a long time before the Caribbean Basin Initiative translated into dollars. Even if it did, most of the money would be in disguised forms of military aid; roads, airfields, that kind of thing. Maybe Sanitex Equipment could hope to sell sanitation equipment to the two or so Air Force bases they were going to build in Honduras.

'Shouldn't we just hold back on this a bit, Mr Chairman? After all, governments we support down there could fall and terrorist groups are targeting American companies. Two American executives were kidnapped in El Salvador last week and there have been other attempts elsewhere, according to this morning's *Times*.'

For once that spoiled brat was saying something intelligent, Lopwitz mused as he scraped out his pipe in the silver ashtray with inscribed corporate logo which he carried with him to board meetings. But to challenge Grover openly instead of opting for a quiet

5

word later showed that young twerp's brashness and lack of tact.

Lopwitz had actually recommended putting John Clark III in the job of Vice President for international sales. The lightweight would soon burn out for the second or third time in his young life and voluntarily leave the company. Now that he was opposing Grover's vision of a Latin American grand tour, the right reasons notwithstanding, John Clark III's demise could come sooner than expected. But it wouldn't do to put his head on the chopping block just yet. The main reason his father retained his interest in the Sanitex Equipment Company was to give this ne'er-do-well son of his some semblance of respectability. If those family shares were sold right now, there were plenty of vultures in Wall Street eager to pay a good price to cannibalize the company. It was the reason Lopwitz had objected to recent suggestions that ownership of the corporation become public. If anybody was going to liquidate Sanitex Equipment, it was going to be him.

'Don't wave the *New York Times* in my face, Mr Clark.' Grover stopped himself. His jowls contracted and his angry demeanor turned into one of mocking humor. 'Are you scared of being kidnapped by a bunch of terrorist wetbacks, Mr Clark?'

Thank God Eddie Hernandez is not around to hear this, Lopwitz was practically whispering to himself as he dipped his empty pipe into the pouch of Jamaican Rum tobacco. That Cuban was the only guy worth a damn in the entire sales division. He had pulled off that Ecuador deal almost entirely on his own. Lopwitz would have suggested his promotion up to New York before if he was not so valuable where he was, but if Grover had now decided to concentrate on Latin America . . .

'I'm not scared of being kidnapped, sir.'

Clark sounded like an aggrieved schoolchild.

Christ, this was easy. Lopwitz packed in the fresh tobacco with his stubby forefinger.

'As Vice President for international sales . . .' Clark now pulled himself together, rather visibly. '. . . I just think that we should wait and see what Washington actually does in Central America and how the situation down there evolves. I realize our company is in trouble. But I sure as hell don't want to see us get into a worse mess by entering into commitments which could literally blow up in our faces. I'm sure our Vice President for government affairs would agree.' Clark launched an urgent look across the table at Bob Riley, someone he'd known from school. Riley had a law degree from New York State University, but hadn't managed to pass his bar examinations. Clark had been instrumental in pushing his résumé to get him the job with Sanitex Equipment that provided the muscular Irishman with a cushy bachelor's life in Washington and a brunette secretary who gave him all he wanted.

Riley, caught off guard, struggled to find a way of pleasing both sides. After some hesitation, he decided on self-cancelling diplomacy. 'I fully agree with your urgent set of priorities, Mr Chairman, and the importance you ascribe to our Latin American market. But there are certain merits in Mr Clark's argument which, in my opinion, may deserve a certain level of consideration.'

Good boy . . . Lopwitz relit the pipe and the fallout of Jamaican Rum tobacco drifted over the conference table. He had come to like Riley even if at first his association with Clark had tended to put him on the gray list. Riley had turned out to be a good front man in Washington. It was Lopwitz's own government contacts which counted.

Grover ignored Riley's guarded words. 'Mr Riley, you will work in Washington to get on the inside track with the State Department and AID. You, Mr Clark,

7

will go to Latin America and we will take the bridge from both ends.'

Clark shot a mean look at Riley, who returned a what–can–I–do–about–it shrug. He then turned to Grover, his back up slightly, his voice a contained monotone. 'Mr Chairman, there are a lot of companies pulling out of Central America right now because of the revolutions going on down there and the dangers they pose to their personnel.'

'That's good news, Mr Clark, we shall have less competition.' Grover leaned his full torso over the table. 'I say damn the torpedoes, full speed ahead.' His right palm slammed down on the table, causing a cloud to lift from Lopwitz's silver ashtray.

Clark had not missed the draft for Vietnam by one year to be used as cannon fodder for his father's bankrupt garbage equipment in some pithole banana republic. 'I will submit a written memorandum explaining my objections to your initiative tomorrow morning, Mr Chairman.'

'And I, Mr Clark, will submit your letter of resignation for your signature and full explanation to your father that his son is too scared of a bunch of rag-tag revolutionaries to help save his own family's company! I hardly think that a decorated hero of the Battle of the Bulge is going to take too kindly to that, Mr Clark.'

All his life, John Clark had not been allowed to forget that his father had been one of General Patton's favorite tank commanders, but he persisted. 'Mr Chairman, if you will allow me. The *New York Times* quotes a Mr James Martin, an expert in terrorism with Security International in Virginia, as saying that Central America is now the most dangerous . . .'

Lopwitz puffed away at his pipe like a contented child with a pacifier, but he was actually starting to get a headache. John Clark's stupidity pitted against Grover's John Wayne act was going beyond the point of amusement. It was also well past the lunch hour and Grover disregarded niceties like providing coffee and sandwiches for such extended occasions. His large stomach was grumbling and during the course of the morning Lopwitz had consumed practically an entire pouch of Jamaican Rum tobacco. But what Clark had said was triggering something in his memory. Terrorists, kidnapping, Security International, James Martin – that was it, the academic who had spoken in that lecture panel for the Council of International Business last summer. Lopwitz had decided to attend at the last moment, having a light schedule that morning. The theme was 'Terrorism and International Business'. First a man from the State Department spoke the usual platitudes and then this Mr Martin, with clipped polished English which bordered on an Oxford accent, gave a world view of the terrorist threat. He had listened to the presentation with the detached amusement with which he might have enjoyed a lecture on Renaissance art. It might have even proved boring were it not for the young man's oratorical gift. Then, during the question and answer period, Lopwitz learned something which had momentarily sparked his imagination, something that made the few thousand dollars which Sanitex Equipment gave the Council annually seem worth it.

Question: Is there some insurance vehicle by which a corporation can protect itself against the kind of threat you have been discussing here, extortion, kidnapping that kind of thing?

The State Department man passed, it was the British accent that answered. 'Yes there is, as a matter of fact. There are policies offered by certain specialized underwriters, Kidnap and Ransom or K & R insurance. Companies can take out these policies on their executives and their families. They guarantee a ransom payment in the event of a kidnapping which is evaluated on the basis of the beneficiary's salary and/

or stake in the company. The ransom is negotiated between the insurer and the kidnappers. Whatever amount is paid does not appear on a corporate balance sheet.'

Tiffany Clark was at her dresser, adding on those last touches of make-up. Just a tiny bit more mascara around the corner of the eyes to hide those incipient wrinkles. She was turning thirty and knew that wrinkles were supposed to start. Had to hurry. John would be home soon and she wanted to be gone by then.

The thought of being with Julio made her shiver. She rubbed her thighs together as she dropped her eye-pencil and inspected the mirror. Her blonde hair was pulled back perfectly straight in a bun, fully exposing her flawlessly proportioned face. Next, her eyes, those ice-blue round eyes that could emit freezing cold or betray steaming heat. She peered closely. No obvious wrinkles yet. She had told Julio that she was only twenty-five. Then her lips. She puckered them. Would he find her just as beautiful this evening? Would he drive into her passionately the way he always did?

She did not know if it was love or lust. Not that she cared. It had begun one late summer weekend when John had stupidly decided to go sailing with the boys. It was a last-minute invitation and she had gone alone. During her five years of marriage, Tiffany had become reluctantly used to the stuffy formality of cocktails and dinners on the Upper East Side. When she walked into the loft in Greenwich Village, the atmosphere was electrifying. In the middle of it all there he was, tall and big and dark, dressed to kill in a loose white suit. Their eyes locked.

The lighting in the loft gave a pink glow. They

drank tequila sunrises and talked a little; they sniffed a couple of lines of coke and when he said he would drive her home, she followed.

Inside his red Ferrari it was impossible to resist. She felt like she was in a warm cloud, as if she had died and come back – so deliciously cheap.

Now she'd follow him to wherever he was from . . . Bolivia, wherever . . . She snapped on her pearl earrings, dabbed on just a touch more lipstick and heard the front door opening. It had to be John. Oh noooo . . . she had always seen Julio during the day, but he wanted her this evening and she just could not say no to him.

Tiffany got up from the dresser, straightened out her black cocktail dress, picked up her purse, checked it for cab fare and decided to confront John with a *fait accompli*. She had stopped feeling any real love for John a year after their wedding. Since his failure on Wall Street he had become increasingly petulant. It had all seemed so perfect when he took her sailing those weekends on Long Island sound, feeling like he was going to conquer the world, and he had proposed to her. It would have been crazy to turn him down. She was tired of living on her meager model's wages, sharing an apartment with three other girls, and the only other proposals she'd had were from old men. She had decided to continue trying to please John but not at the expense of her true happiness. She had inherited some money recently, anyway.

When she reached the entrance hall he was in the adjacent living-room getting himself a drink. He seemed haggard. She would try her best to make a dash for it. 'Oh, hi honey, I'm just going out.'

He didn't look up from the far end of the living-room, busy unscrewing a bottle of Jack Daniels. 'I need to talk to you, Tif.'

'Not now, baby, I'm going to be late.' Something was wrong and she didn't care to find out . . .

11

especially if it had anything whatsoever to do with the Sanitex Equipment Corporation. Or could it just be . . . She held her breath.

'I may be leaving the company.'

She could barely conceal a sigh of relief, trying to sound sincere. 'Oh, darling, that's terrible. Tell me about it when I get back.' She went to the coat closet.

'Tif, I need to talk to you now. I just had one of the worst goddam days in my life and . . .' He turned to look at her. She had managed to slip into a long rain-coat, but it could not conceal the fact that she was made up to gatecrash a royal dinner party.

'Just where are you going that's so important?' He walked to the middle of the living-room.

She closed the coat closet and opened the front door to the elevator landing which they shared with another apartment. 'Oh nothing, honey, I just have to meet my modelling agent about a possible new contract. I won't be long.' She would have to cut short her evening with Julio.

'At this hour?'

'He originally made the appointment for earlier but called to say something unexpected had come up and could I see him after hours. I didn't know that there would be any . . .'

'Well call him up and postpone it again until tomorrow, goddamit, I need to talk to you.'

'I can't call him because we're meeting at a studio where it'll be hard to page him.' She had become expert at lying.

He walked towards her. 'At a *studio*? Tif, I could be out of a job, now just stay a while and make him wait.'

He was getting on her nerves. Her own lies not withstanding, the job at Sanitex Equipment didn't mean anything to him. He just wanted some sympathy because he'd obviously been dragged through the mud by those monsters Grover and Lopwitz. They had plenty of private income to live on and she felt like saying, 'I'm sure Daddy will fix it up for you dear', but thought better of it. Instead, she said, icily, 'If you are going to be out of a job, then I shouldn't lose an opportunity to make a bit of extra cash.' Thank God she had thought of the right excuse. 'I'll have a nice surprise in store for you when I get back.' She didn't know whether to give him a reassuring kiss or just rush out the door. In the middle of her indecision, he got in front of her and leaned casually on the open door with an outstretched arm, barring her way.

'Since when do you go for a meeting with an agent in a studio wearing a cocktail dress? Are we going anywhere later?'

She gave it all she could, pretending not to notice his sarcasm. But her eyes were all ice. 'If you like. You've always said I look my best in a cocktail dress and . . .'

'Where are you really going, Tif?'

Oh God. 'I've told you where I'm going. Now will you please let me through. I'm going to be late, it's raining outside and it will be difficult to get a cab.'

She was just short enough to slip under his arm into the landing. She pressed the elevator button, hoping to God that it would hurry up.

'Get back into the apartment, Tif.' His voice was rising.

'Sorry, honey, I have to go.'

'Get back into the goddam apartment!'

She just stared straight ahead and heard herself saying, 'I have a right to my own life, John,' despite her fear that he would come out to grab her. The elevator slid open. He started towards her, screaming, 'I don't know what other sonovabitch is getting into your little pants but you are staying here if I have to – ' and Mr and Mrs Cannon, the respectable middle-aged couple from across the hall, walked out of their apartment.

Their shocked expressions stopped John cold. Tiffany slipped into the elevator and the door slid shut.

'So how did you leave things with the Prince of Wales?' The mocking reference to John Clark III had become a private joke between Lopwitz and Grover. The General Counsel was having an early morning meeting with Grover to find out the results of yesterday's private session with Clark.

'Not too differently from the way we left it at the management meeting, Herb.' The Chairman was pacing behind his desk, in front of the large twelfth-floor window. The din of Park Avenue's rush-hour traffic was barely audible.

Grover was nervous. He didn't want a confrontation with the Clark family. He was not actually certain that the ex-CEO would see things his way. But he sure as hell couldn't let that useless whippersnapper overturn his decisions.

Lopwitz lit his pipe. 'Do you think he's going to stay?'

'I don't know for sure, Herb. He got down to trying to compromise on going to some countries and not others. But I made it clear to him that unless he was willing to go to all of them, I wanted his resignation this morning. He said that he would discuss it with his wife. My gut feeling is that he will probably leave.'

His wife, Lopwitz chuckled to himself, that horny bitch. He had the full scoop on her comings and goings with that South American playboy, whoever the hell he was. All of New York knew about it, except possibly John Clark III. Well, at least if it was up to her, Grover should not have any trouble packing him off on a long business trip to Latin America. That much was good news.

'Have you considered offering him some kind of

14

incentive, like a raise in salary?' Lopwitz continued.

Grover stopped pacing. 'Hell, Herb, we're facing cost overruns and possible bankruptcy and you're suggesting that we offer him a raise just to go on a trip to Latin America when Hernandez can do as good a job on his own? I just·thought John would add some decorative presence, representing the company's ownership. I honestly didn't think he would object or I wouldn't have even proposed it. Hell, if necessary I'll go myself. I'm not afraid of getting kidnapped.'

That word again. While Grover met with Clark yesterday afternoon, Lopwitz had put a call through to Security International and had set up a tentative appointment with James Martin for later in the week.

'Come now, Howard.' Lopwitz fiddled with his pipe. 'I don't want a confrontation with the Clark family any more than you do. Besides, I think a tour of Latin America might do the boy some good. Old man Clark would surely be pleased if his son agreed to go and, well, a hundred thousand dollars here and there can't make much of a difference at this stage of the game.'

'A hundred thousand dol . . . Herb, that boy makes more private income than his current salary, by how much do you propose I raise it?'

'I propose you double it.'

John Clark III was sitting in his swivel chair turned about-face from his desk. His feet were crossed on top of the radiator as he looked out of his office window and down the narrow gorge of high-rises into 51st Street. He was washing down his second aspirin that morning with a cup of coffee his secretary had brought him. He had woken up with a headache, and for the first time he could remember was glad to have an office to which he could escape. His scene with

Tiffany in front of their neighbors, people he was trying to cultivate, felt like the most humiliating experience of his adult life. Immediately afterwards, he had gone through Tiffany's address book for the number of her modelling agent. When he rang, Cruickshank was still at his office, and could only tell him that there was no new modelling contract for Tiffany, nor did he know of any work she could be engaged in through anyone else. 'She has not done any modelling for over a year, Mr Clark,' he said, as if to imply that she was no longer taken seriously in his professional circles.

John Clark now knew for certain that the rumors about his wife were true. She was having an affair, and from the looks of it a pretty intense one. As he drank three-quarters of a bottle of bourbon that night, Clark had reluctantly come to the conclusion that going on the trip was not such a bad idea after all. The possible dangers were outweighed by the prospect of being caught between a scandalous separation from his wife and a ruined career in his father's own company, for reasons that his family might not approve. He needed a way out, even if it meant joining the Foreign Legion. Maybe Tiffany's affair would have spent itself by the time he got back. If, on the other hand, a divorce was necessary, he would need all the moral support he could get.

Clark had gone to sleep in the apartment's second bedroom, the one he had been keeping reserved for the child which Tiffany had consistently put off having. When he woke up this morning feeling like death warmed over, he peeked into the master bedroom to find that Tiffany had not come back at all.

Who could it be? he had wondered to himself as he got dressed for work, deciding to wear his gold-button blazer that day instead of a suit. Jealousy gave way to impotence, the sinking sensation of being unmanned as he realized that he had lost his power over her, that she now belonged to someone else.

He had practically decided to go up to see Grover and agree to the trip when the intercom on his desk buzzed. It was the Chairman – without the usual brusqueness. 'Would you like to come up if you've got a minute, John, there is something I would like to propose to you before we discuss your decision.'

Grover received him in a fatherly manner, asking his secretary to bring in some coffee. After some brief observations about the lousy weather, as if implying that it had something to do with his rotten mood the day before, he went on to ask, 'Did you talk things over with your wife?'

Clark groped for an answer. 'There was something of a family emergency yesterday evening and we really didn't get the chance to talk.'

'Oh, sorry to hear that, nothing serious I hope?'

'No, nothing serious.' Clark's eyes watered. In his attempt to be the concerned family friend, Grover had just picked at his fresh wounds.

'Well, that's good, John, now let me get to the point. I talked with Herb earlier this morning and he is of the opinion that there are certain risks involved in what we are asking you to undertake for us in Latin America, so we have decided to compensate for that by allowing you a very substantial raise in salary. I would be willing to take the unprecedented step of doubling your current intake and increasing your stock options in the company if you will agree to go to all the countries I choose. Is that a deal?'

2

Lopwitz got out of his cab when it reached the corner of King Street and Royal, and walked the remaining half block. He had flown down to Virginia that morning from New York on the ten o'clock Eastern Shuttle to National Airport, minutes away by taxi from the center of Alexandria. The brass plaque outside the brick town house read Security International. Lopwitz pressed the doorbell.

He was greeted by a polite secretary, attractive for her middle years, who ushered him through a narrow corridor and up a flight of stairs to the second floor that opened into a spacious room. There was a computer and a desk buried in paper, behind which the man he had come to see was standing to welcome him in rolled-up shirtsleeves.

'Mr Martin, I presume.' They shook hands.

'How do you do, Mr Lopwitz, please sit down.' He had a ready smile with the brisk manner and understated arrogance of a man in authority. But so young, not more than thirty, and that clipped accent. Couldn't be an ex-spook. College professor, maybe. But again, so young and there was no sign of a degree certificate. Lopwitz was having lunch with his contact at the CIA to get the lowdown on this mysterious celebrity.

He took off his Burberry and folded it over the back of his chair. 'Thank you very much for taking the time to meet with me, Mr Martin.' Since Lopwitz did not have a totally clear idea who or what he was really meeting, he decided to treat him the way he would a specialized lawyer.

'My pleasure, I'm very glad you could come by.' Martin sat back down.

Clearly, not that many people did. Martin was slender and hungry-looking. Lopwitz would start with some flattery. 'I saw you quoted in the *Times* the other day and remembered that presentation you gave last July at the Council of International Business. You did a good job.'

A slight laugh. 'I'm glad somebody thinks so.'

The charm was there but the modesty was not. 'I understand that your company puts out an information service.'

'That's right, the Security Risk Assessment. We analyze security threats posed worldwide by terrorist activity. Our objective is to assess the degree of risk it poses to government stability, economic interests and corporate assets in different countries. We look closely at countries affected by terrorism and develop perspectives on the level of threat they face. We also examine the infrastructure of terrorist groups, their international connections, their degree of grass-roots support, their state backing in cases in which they are acting extra-officially. Based on information we bank in our computer, we can draw projections on terrorist targeting patterns and are increasingly able to anticipate major terrorist attacks.'

Lopwitz liked the sales pitch. It was a well-rehearsed delivery, the use of jargon was balanced. Despite the bizarre nature of his subject, Martin made it sound reassuringly banal. 'How much does this information service of yours cost?'

'Two thousand dollars a year.'

'How many clients do you have?'

'About sixty or seventy corporations and some government agencies.'

Lopwitz took out his checkbook and started to

write one out. 'I make it payable to Security International?'

'Why, yes.' Martin was pleasantly surprised. No one had ever written out a check for his service without undergoing lengthy bureaucratic procedures in which everyone has to say yes and anyone can say no.

'Here you are, I want to start receiving it at my office.' Lopwitz handed over the check accompanied by his business card. 'I'll tell you the reason I've come here, Mr Martin. We are sending one of our top people to visit various countries in Latin America, particularly around Central America and the Caribbean. We are naturally concerned about his safety. Can you give me a situation report on these countries?' Lopwitz produced a typed list from his inside breast pocket and gave it to Martin.

'It reads like a list of places where not to go: El Salvador, Guatemala, Honduras, Panama, Costa Rica, Dominican Republic, Colombia. That's practically all Indian country, Mr Lopwitz.'

'I realize. I would like to have one of those detailed perspectives you mentioned, by tomorrow morning, if that's possible?'

'That's rather short notice but we can probably manage. There's an extra charge, you realize.'

'How much?'

'Let's say, one thousand dollars.'

'I'll pay you on receipt. Now, Mr Martin, let me ask you some more questions . . . is there an additional consulting fee for taking up your morning?'

'Two hundred an hour.'

'I'll pay you for two and a half hours.' Lopwitz, who had not let go of his checkbook, wrote out another for five hundred dollars. 'It's made out to you.'

Could this be Santa Claus? Martin thought to himself as he was handed the check.

'Now, what I want to know is the following. These

countries where terrorist organizations are . . .' He searched for the right word.

'Are active,' interjected Martin.

'Yes, that's right, are active. In these countries where terrorist organizations are active, I can understand that there is a very real threat to business executives who are residents or work there for any length of time. But what is the likelihood that something would happen to one who was just going in for a few days?'

'They are less likely to be targeted, of course, but it certainly happens. Two engineers from a company in California were kidnapped in El Salvador just last week and they were only there on a brief visit to inspect a plant. A Vice President of Texaco was nabbed in Honduras, in the first recent kidnapping of a foreign executive to take place in that country, and he had only been there a couple of days. He was abducted from the parking lot of his hotel. Terrorist organizations today are developing very extensive surveillance techniques and intelligence capabilities, especially in regions of protracted low-intensity conflict.'

Now the jargon was making Lopwitz feel semiliterate. 'Let me ask you another question. To carry out a kidnapping, as you say, a terrorist group needs substantial . . . support . . . Is that the correct way of putting it?'

'Infrastructure.'

'Infrastructure, right, it needs some substantial infrastructure. Now, for a group to have this kind of infrastructure it would have needed to be around for a while. It would be expected to have an . . . established presence.'

'Highly active long-term presence.'

'Thank you, Mr Martin, a highly active long-term presence. Would it be likely or possible, in your opinion, that some new group no one would have

21

heard of before, without a highly active long-term presence, could suddenly emerge to kidnap a foreign executive? I ask you this because I'm sure the reports you will give me tomorrow will contain an alphabet soup of terrorist groups known to have a highly active long-term presence. But I just wonder if an unexpected threat can develop?'

'Yes, absolutely. In the murky world of terrorism it is so difficult to tell who is actually who most of the time anyway. I reckon that's the reason this company is in business.' He leaned back in his chair and looked briefly upwards as he stretched his elbows, putting his hands behind his head. 'Known terrorist organizations are themselves very often no more than umbrella names for separately structured semi-autonomous cells. This varies, but certainly in many of the Latin American urban guerrilla organizations, separate cells of five to ten members each are tightly compartmentalized. Members of one cell are not allowed to know the identity of members of another cell to maintain operational security for the rest of the organization. Separate cells may claim their actions using different names. This has a psychological effect of making it seem that a revolutionary movement is more widespread than it actually is, and is a good way of confusing the authorities. There are often internecine quarrels between separate cells, cross-pollination with other groups, splinter factions, spin-offs from one group who go to form their own group under a separate command structure. And, of course, in situations of protracted activity new terrorist groups are forming and recycling all the time.'

He now had his hands on his desk and looked directly at Lopwitz, who for his part was doing his best to take in this lecture on terrorist biology.

'Actually,' he continued, 'the surest way for a new or a starting group to gain high-profile revolutionary

22

credibility, as well as funding to expand its operations, is by kidnapping a foreign corporate executive. This guarantees it publicity as a force against the capitalist imperialist foe as well as assuring a ransom payment, since companies are far more likely to buy back their hostages than, say, a government.'

Lopwitz had lit his pipe.

'The kidnappings that I mentioned to you before of the two American engineers in El Salvador and the Texaco executive in Honduras were committed by a group with a very limited track record, Partido Revolucionario de Trabajadores Centro Americano, PRTC. I looked into it and found that the only actions it had previously claimed were a couple of small-scale bombings in San Salvador. There is actually nothing that unusual in what you are suggesting, Mr Lopwitz.'

There was no doubt that Martin really knew his subject, perhaps a bit too well. 'Another question. What would be the chances that a company like mine, without very high visibility, would get hit?'

'You would naturally have much more to fear if you were IBM. But to give you the most recent example, the two Americans kidnapped in El Salvador worked for a mid-sized electronics company in California, not a very well-known firm internationally. It is not listed in the *Fortune Five Hundred*.'

'So from what you are telling me the extent of risk to the man we are planning to send down there is considerable.'

'I would say that's correct.'

'In your lecture at the Council of International Business you mentioned insurance of a certain kind, Kidnapping and Ransom it's called if I am not mistaken. How does one go about securing one of these policies?'

'At Lloyds, that's where you find the only underwriters who deal in this.' Martin reached into his drawer, pulled out a card and handed it to Lopwitz. 'Please tell Ian I referred you.'

'I certainly will, Mr Martin. And thank you very much for your help. I expect that we will soon be back in touch.'

When Lopwitz had left, Martin put his feet up on his desk and reclined in his swivel chair. He felt pleased with his own performance and looked at the five hundred dollar check made in his name which Lopwitz had left him. He should enter it into the company's account. But there was that stunning blonde reporter who had come to his office the other day whom he was supposed to be taking out tonight, and he was down to less than fifty dollars until pay-day.

Lopwitz was in an exterior elevator on his way to one of the top floors of the Lloyds building, an ultra-modern steel and glass monstrosity that shot up from a narrow side-street in the heart of London's financial district, or 'The City'. It blended into the architecture around it like an arrival from another planet. Despite having rested for a day, Lopwitz still felt jet-lagged. By the time he reached the offices of Hedge & Corbit on the thirty-fourth floor he also had vertigo. Lopwitz dizzily entered the brokerage offices and was ushered into a conference room which also offered a pano-ramic sweep over the River Thames. He sat down with his back to the view, awaiting the arrival of the most exotic type of insurance broker that he could possibly ever meet.

In came Ian Whitecliff, tall, sandy-haired, in his early forties, an ex-officer of the Queen's Fusiliers. Though full of apologies for making him wait, Whitecliff had that breezy style and distinctly English freezing politeness. In his elegantly rumpled Savile

Row pinstripe he looked somewhat out of place at the pinnacle of this science fiction colossus.

'I believe that we are the only ones in this building who continue our English custom of serving sherry at this time of the day.' It was just before lunch. 'Would you care for a snifter?'

Lopwitz never drank during the day, but could not pass up a chance to drink sherry at the top of Lloyds of London. 'A small one, thank you.'

Whitecliff pressed a button and a bosomy pink-cheeked young secretary instantly popped through the door to take the order.

They exchanged a few more pleasantries. Lopwitz asked if he could smoke and produced the pipe.

The sherries arrived. They toasted and took their first sips.

'Well, what can we do for you, Mr Lopwitz? Sanitex Equipment, I believe your company is called.'

'Yes, that's quite correct. I understand that you broker a certain specialized type of insurance that my company may need. We are sending one of our top people on a swing through various countries which could be rather dangerous from the standpoint of his personal security.'

'You are referring to our Kidnapping and Ransom policy.'

'Yes, that's quite correct.' Lopwitz lit his pipe and spoke between his teeth. 'I would be interested to find out how exactly it is you write such policies.' He sucked in the flame of his Zippo lighter.

'Well, Mr Lopwitz, let me begin by asking you to briefly forget all you have ever known about insurance.' His demeanor suddenly changed to that of paratroop commander briefing a suicide mission. Lopwitz had taken the time to research Whitecliff's background. On his impeccable military record there was one year of active service which was blank. In the

British army this could mean nothing else except duty with the SAS.

'Many people who come here believe that K & R is some kind of life-insurance policy. It is not. The coverage only takes effect in the event of a kidnapping and then only for a ransom. If the beneficiary dies or is killed while in captivity, the insurance does not cover. In such cases what would happen is that the underwriters negotiate some relatively small compensation with the company for direct damages or losses resulting from the incident. This is part of our extortion coverage clause. I need to make this absolutely clear.' He waited for a reaction.

'I understand, Mr Whitecliff, please continue.'

'Now, another way in which this policy differs from most others is in estimating the coverage.'

Lopwitz was intrigued.

'There is no sure way of determining how much ransom is going to be demanded in the event of a kidnapping. If you are insuring a car or an oil tanker, you can arrive at a pretty accurate estimate of the maximum damage or loss which may be incurred. But when you are insuring an individual against ransom which some unknown group of criminals or terrorists are going to demand, you really can't count on any exactitude. The highest ransom that was ever paid was fifty million dollars to a terrorist group in Argentina. But other than making the *Guinness Book of Records*, this case really has little bearing on what can happen currently. In other words, each policy has to be tailored individually.'

Whitecliff paused. Lopwitz kept puffing on his pipe.

'In cases where the beneficiary of a K & R policy is more or less stationary in a given location where he is likely to be targeted by a particular group, it may be possible to assess his coverage based on the capabilities or precedents set by terrorists or criminals operating in that particular area. We have recently written some policies for major industrialists in the Basque region of the north of Spain, for instance, where the separatist guerrilla organization ETA runs a highly organized kidnapping and extortion syndicate. This has been unusually easy, because ETA, we found, calculates what it calls 'revolutionary taxes' in a highly systematized fashion, rather like an Inland Revenue. They study an individual's income and net worth, basing their extortion demands on informed calculations. Most other terrorist groups are not quite so tidy or, dare I use the word, scrupulous. There are many more cases in which the situation is quite the opposite. In many parts of Latin America, for example, terrorists tend to have a spiralling effect on the price of ransoms. During a kidnapping campaign by Marxist urban guerrilla groups against foreign executives in Brazil some twenty years ago, ransom demands which began in the low single millions of dollars, escalated to the tens of millions in a matter of months, quite irrespective of the seniority or net worth of the individuals being traded. It was simply a reaction by the terrorist groups to the success of their kidnappings. A similar thing is occurring today in El Salvador. So in cases such as yours in which your man is going to be traveling, any coverage we set is quite arbitrary. Are we clear on that point?'

Lopwitz nodded.

'Now, to a third point.' A slight smirk lit Whitecliff's face. 'The ransom is only paid if we can firmly establish the identity of the kidnappers.'

Lopwitz snuggled more deeply into his seat.

'There have been cases of kidnapping involving anonymous extortionists in which the insurance company has refused to cover the ransom. But in practically all incidents committed by an identifiable terrorist group or a known crime syndicate, the coverage goes into effect. Our underwriters have specialized consultants to assess the kidnapping. If they determine that the threat is credible, the insurance company offers to cover.'

'It's my understanding, Mr Whitecliff, that in some of these very unstable countries, terrorist groups with little or no track record may suddenly appear and take someone hostage. How do you evaluate the credibility of the kidnappers in those cases?'

'Well, I suppose that we can never be a hundred percent certain, Mr Lopwitz. As I said, a team is sent to inspect the case. Sometimes they can count on the cooperation of local authorities, other times they can't. It's easier of course if they can. But as I told you, in almost every case which involves, how should I put it, recognizable terrorists, the insurance can be counted on to pay the ransom.'

Lopwitz scraped out his pipe into a large glass ash-tray that Whitecliff pushed his way. 'What are the premiums?'

'Well, that naturally depends on the coverage we settle on, of course. But offhand, I don't think your case has that high a risk factor . . .'

Lopwitz was glad to hear that in this aspect, Whitecliff was contradicting Martin of Security International.

'Your company tends to have rather low visibility, does it not? The man you are sending is not particularly well known?' Whitecliff looked inquiringly at Lopwitz.

'He is our Vice President of international sales. His father is the ex-Chairman of the Board.'

'Shouldn't make that much difference. He's traveling through, not likely to remain in any single location for much over a month?' Whitecliff rubbed his chin speculatively.

'That's right.'

'No. I don't think your premiums should be particularly high. What cover do you want?'

'What's the maximum I can get?'

'Let me see, this chap's family is involved with the company, you say?'

'Between him and his parents, they own half the shares.'

'That does put him in a rather high category.' Whitecliff jotted down some notes and figures on a white pad. 'What's your company worth, about?'

'Over one hundred million dollars. Do you need annual turnover?'

'That won't be necessary.'

Lopwitz was relieved.

'His salary is in the six digits?'

'One hundred and fifty thousand a year, not counting his personal income.'

Whitecliff lifted his eyebrows slightly. 'Yes, I would say he is close to our top category. His coverage should be above ten million. Fifteen million, at least.'

'He is very valuable to us, I must have thirty million.'

'That's a bit high.'

'Twenty-five million, nothing less.'

'A tad below that, Mr Lopwitz. On principle we could agree on twenty-four million.'

Lopwitz sipped the last of his sherry and turned to face the Thames. Things were falling into place.

3

Dick Stewart was a high-level operative for the CIA. He had been generously rewarded for the occasional covert job he did for the Sanitex Equipment Corporation, advising who to bribe where and most recently arranging for a secret kickback to an Arab government. Thanks to Herbert Lopwitz, Stewart could look forward to retiring as a wealthy man. He was now sitting to lunch with Lopwitz at the International Club on K Street, the business section of the nation's capital, where lawyers, lobbyists, academic think-tankers and public relations entrepreneurs gambled at the influence game just a few blocks from the White House.

'So what can you tell me about him?' Lopwitz dipped his spoon into the cold vichyssoise. When he had mentioned the name of James Martin to Stewart during their last lunch before he left for London, the CIA man was unfamiliar with it. Since then, Stewart had done some digging.

'Well, good and bad.' Stewart picked at his mixed salad.

'Tell me the good first.'

'He is good at what he does. The Security Risk Assessment is read by our boys down in Analysis.'

Down in Analysis. Lopwitz was amused by the automatic superiority which the Agency's field men assumed over the thinkers in the basement.

'They find it quite helpful.'

'So he really has credibility.'

'Yes, in his narrow field he has credibility.'

30

'How did he get into this narrow field?'

'He started out as a journalist. Did a lot of work for the London *Foreign Review*, covering the situation in Portugal when they had that revolution there and that shaky period in Spain following Franco's death.'

'Speak Spanish?'

'Fluently, and French and Portuguese. He has a great facility for getting information. He penetrates quite well. In Portugal, he managed to get the whole scoop on an underground network that was forming among supporters of the old military dictatorship. Got the intricate details. He might as well have led the whole goddam conspiracy himself.'

'Do you guys use him?'

'We have without his knowledge. In Madrid, the guys at our Embassy put him on to a story which proved conveniently embarrassing to the opposition. He made a few enemies. Had to come back here afterwards. We never contacted him directly. Instead, some people he was speaking to at State were encouraged to steer him in the right direction. When this former army intelligence colonel formed Security International, he was picked. As I said, his reports are useful to our analysis people.'

'Why don't you bring him inside?'

'It's been proposed, but he is considered too entrepreneurial, also kind of arrogant and undisciplined. Won't finish his degree, gets into personal problems, wants things his way. You know, the basic prima donna. They don't like guys like that at Langley, not any more. A normal kid who waited on tables through college and was a good student is far more their type these days. Martin is fine where he is as far as they are concerned.'

Lopwitz noticed how Stewart had switched from we to they as if not wanting to be fully identified with questionable practices.

'What's his financial situation?'

'Lives from pay check to pay check. Gets maybe three to four hundred a week plus bonuses and commissions from clients he brings in. Does a bit on the side for State. But it's still hardly enough for his apartment and his five-year-old Buick.'

Lopwitz enjoyed what he was hearing. 'Married or engaged?'

'Definitely not married and not engaged as far as we know.'

'Not queer, is he?'

'Hell no. He spends half his life chasing girls. Not that he gets that many of them, that's part of the problem. One of our girls tested him out once.' Stewart leaned over, his voice dropped to a loud whisper. 'He's a horny bastard.'

Martin slammed the phone down. She had turned him down again, goddamit! She had an excuse last weekend and a different one for this weekend. Was he trying too hard? Did she have someone else? Maybe he was getting some kind of reputation. It all seemed to go so well when he took Jane Winter for dinner last Friday. She had told him to call her the next day and when he did the excuses started. So much for the rising star of *NBN News*.

Martin checked his watch. It was five-thirty. He needed a drink. As he started to slip on his herringbone jacket his phone buzzed. It was the secretary's gentle voice. 'A lady for you on line two, Mr Martin.'

'Thank you, Mary Ellen.' He pressed down the illuminated button beneath the dial. Maybe she had changed her mind. 'Hello.'

'Hi, is this James Martin?'

It was a soft, tingling voice. He sat back down and leaned forward on his desk. 'Yes.'

'Oh listen, sorry to bother you, my name is Lisa.'

There was friendly humor in her words. 'I'm a friend of Herb Lopwitz. He said he talked to you last week? Well . . . I'm an International Relations major at Georgetown and . . . oh, this is so embarrassing.' She giggled, then composed herself just slightly. 'I'm writing a paper on terrorism and Herb told me that you . . . well, that you are a real expert.'

'That was kind of Herb.'

'I'm wondering . . . would it be . . . would it please be possible for us two to meet.' It was like she was on her knees. 'I really need your help.'

Martin could not believe it. 'Sure . . . When?' It came out like a loud whisper.

'I need to turn it in by next week.' Her voice was more relaxed now and she was practically cooing into the line. 'How about this evening?'

From the moment they had met for drinks a few hours ago, Martin and Lisa had gotten along like a house on fire. She said she was twenty. Aside from her terrific looks and her great sense of humor, among her other great qualities was a total fascination with him and his work. 'You mean I'm actually having dinner with a terrorist?' she giggled in the cozy Italian restaurant on M Street, a hand girlishly poised over her mouth in mock shock.

Back at her studio apartment, just a few blocks away in the middle of Georgetown, she invited him up – to look at her paper, of course. She had resisted a bit at first, as was natural. But once he had her blouse unbuttoned and was feeling her erect nipples, it didn't take long before he was unzipping her tight jeans.

Now, her head was tossing from side to side, chestnut hair everywhere, legs bent and wide apart as she screamed towards an orgasm, that primeval yell coming from deep inside of her. Her body untensed and he lingered inside her.

Afterwards, when they lay together, she snuggled

up, caressed his right tricep and gently licked his jaw. 'You are such a strong lover . . . and a terrorist.' She burst into a giggle, tossing her head back on the pillow. 'You can stay with me for as long as you want. I'm all alone, you know.'

James Martin briskly ascended the wide marble staircase up to the second-floor lounge of the Cosmos Club, two steps at a time. His thumbs were sticking out of the hip pockets of his navy-blue blazer as he spotted Lopwitz sitting in a comfortable leather sofa in a far corner browsing through the *Washington Post*. It was just before five p.m. They were the only ones in Washington's best gentleman's club. Lopwitz gestured at getting up as Martin approached. They shook hands. Martin took an armchair.

He looks like a dog that's just eaten raw steak, Lopwitz mused to himself. 'I understand you got together with Lisa.'

'Yes, we got together over the weekend . . . to work on her paper. Great girl. Thanks a lot for your good word.'

'Don't mention it. Yes, she is a very nice girl, Lisa, a friend of my daughter's. I also know her parents. I take her out to lunch every once in a while when I come to town. She told me she had this paper to write so I naturally . . .'

'You definitely did the right thing, Mr Lopwitz.'

'Please call me Herb. She gave me a call yesterday. She rather seems to like you.'

'That's always good to know.' Martin betrayed a wink.

'Good, good.' Lopwitz put his pipe down. 'Now, Martin, I've been looking over those situation reports you gave me.' He pulled them out of the briefcase next to him. 'I'm rather concerned about the Dominican Republic. Our man should be spending quite a lot of time down there. You say, and I quote you, "Terrorist activity can be expected to intensify in urban areas in the near future. A major kidnapping targeting an American or other foreign executive could precede a full-scale offensive by the Ejercito de Liberacion Dominicano" – he struggled through the Spanish pronunciation – "following the pattern set by other Cuban-supported guerrilla organizations seeking to overthrow established governments in the region.'

'That's right.'

'Martin, I would like to retain you to go down to the Dominican Republic for me.'

He would love to. But Martin had to seem guarded to maintain professional appearances. Lopwitz was really a godsend. First he signs up for the service. Then he fixes him up with an absolutely dynamite chick. And now he is offering him, possibly, the most exciting assignment he has been given in years. 'What exactly is it that you would want me to do?'

'I want you to prepare a first-hand report of the terrorist threat down there. I want detailed profiles on terrorist groups operating in the country, particularly in the capital, Santo Domingo. I've kept in mind very closely what you said about the way in which kidnapping an American businessman is the fastest way for a new group to gain funding and "revolutionary credibility", I believe you call it. You should concentrate not just on the ELD, but on splinter factions and any new groups that could be emerging. I want you to do some real penetrating and actually talk to some of these guys. Are you up to it?'

Martin was struck by a combination of thrill and apprehension, as if he was about to descend on a steep roller-coaster. 'Yes . . . I suppose so . . . I mean of course. But we will have to discuss it with my principals.'

'That's another thing, Martin, there are certain reasons why I want you to undertake this outside your company's channels. Can you take a leave of absence?' From the recordings he had heard of Martin's conversations in Lisa's apartment, Lopwitz knew he had over a month's vacation time saved up. 'I'm going to need you for an entire month. I'll pay you five hundred dollars a day plus expenses and a good bonus when the job is over. Can you be ready to go in ten days?'

4

The uniformed officer at the Control booth stamped through the American passport with the name of Douglas Weinstein. The rotund man in tropical suit, sunglasses and Panama hat made his way through the demonstrative throngs of friends and relatives who were greeting passengers off the flight from Miami. He was carrying a thinly packed suitbag slung over his shoulder and an attaché case. He had taken both pieces on board the plane as hand luggage. He now jostled, pipe clamped firmly in his mouth, through the hugs, kisses and affectionate exclamations of a large Dominican family fawning over the return of what one would guess to be a prodigal daughter.

As Lopwitz emerged into the sun-drenched steambath of the Caribbean day a taxi pulled up for him. The drive into Santo Domingo was pleasant enough, down a well-kept highway lined by palm trees that ran along the edge of the tropical bay. Lopwitz made mental notes of what he had to do. He would check into the Hotel Lima before going to the lunch that his friend Dick Stewart had helped to arrange, using some private contacts, with the Chief of Police of Santo Domingo.

As the taxi entered the capital, the boulevard became La Avenida de la Independencia, starting in the slum districts that ringed Santo Domingo with the squalor of most growing Latin American cities. Rough cement apartment blocks along the Avenida gave way to side-streets of rickety slab-wood houses.

They crossed a bridge which the cab driver announced was the point of heaviest combat when President Johnson landed the Marines in 1965 to forestall 'another Cuba'. Over the side, the worst of the slums were visible. Dirt-colored shanty towns of over-crowded, makeshift shacks terraced the slopes down to the water's edge. Once over the bridge, the city was bustling. New constructions provided ample wall space for political graffiti, giving the first hints that the specter of another Cuba threatened again.

'Yankee go home' was painted in man-sized letters along about ten yards of cement. A bit further, a woman balancing a fruit basket on her head walked past *Viva la Revolucion*. *Abajo con el Imperialismo* was sprayed in red over the billboard of a bikini-clad blonde advertizing suntan lotion. *El Pueblo Armado Nuca Sera Vencido* occupied the entire exterior of a store competing for attention with the Coca-Cola sign. *Con Cuba Para Siempre* was a few doors down. Lopwitz noticed that painted beneath most of the slogans was the signature of the ELD, Ejercito de Liberacion Dominicano.

According to the taxi driver there had been a serious riot just a few nights ago further down the Avenida, in the more affluent section where they were heading. A mob had congregated in front of the modern opera house being inaugurated with a concert in honor of President Camuñas, the luster-less figurehead of the Partido Popular del Progresso – the only party to win elections in the Dominican Republic in two decades. Snipers hidden in the crowd opened fire on police and troops as they moved to disperse it. A fifty-caliber machine gun mounted on an army jeep then opened up on the demonstrators, killing about a dozen.

As the taxi wound around La Plaza de la Indepen-dencia Lopwitz noticed the boarded-up windows, and black spots on the pavement marking where cars had been burned. They pulled up at his hotel, just a block away from the new opera house.

Lopwitz presented himself at the reception desk, where a message from Colonel Ventura awaited him with instructions on where to go for their lunch. Up in his room he helped himself to an ice-cold beer and relaxed for a few minutes admiring the fourth-floor view of the swimming pool. The usual midday crowd of tourists and affluent Santo Domingans was assembling. The Dominican women, in fashionable Brazilian tanga bikinis, were invariably beautiful. Lopwitz finished the last of his beer, fixed his necktie and left for the meeting carrying his suit jacket and the attaché case.

Colonel Ventura stood up to greet Lopwitz in the small private dining-room he reserved for such occasions in the Club Colonial, a gray stone building in the historic section of Santo Domingo. He was wearing civilian clothes with a loose-fitting white guayabera, the thinly woven shirt with breast and side pockets worn outside trousers, the traditional business-wear in the Spanish Caribbean. Ventura had ordered them a meal of fresh sole. A chilled bottle of white wine arrived inside a silver ice bucket. The waiter poured them each a glass and they toasted.

'So what brings you to Santo Domingo, Mr Weinstein? I understand you have some important matters to discuss with me.' Ventura could not get away from his official manner even if a slight nervousness showed he wanted to. He also knew Lopwitz's real name, but respected the basic precaution against hidden tape recorders. It was also a password to Lopwitz, who knew that he knew, to start edging towards the discreet business at hand. The fish arrived.

'Colonel, I proceed on the understanding that what I say here is strictly off the record since what I would like to propose could greatly be to your benefit, should you agree to my conditions.'

'You have my word of honor that nothing said here goes beyond this room.'

Lopwitz knew that a person's word of honor meant something in the Latin world, in spite of what he was about to propose. 'Someone representing my company will be coming to Santo Domingo soon, within the next month.'

Ventura nodded, deboning his sole.

'A kidnapping could occur.'

Ventura sipped his wine and looked at Lopwitz. He could hardly disagree. The ELD might move soon, even if no one had been taken yet.

'I could use your help.'

Did he want special protection? That would be simple enough to arrange. Ventura betrayed a slight sense of disappointment; it wouldn't mean much money for him. He sipped more wine and kept silent.

'If you cooperate with me on this matter I can provide you with the safest investment you could possibly have and something that may prove rather useful in view of the way things are moving in your country.'

Ventura had accepted bribes before from the kind of people from whom one is supposed to accept bribes: corporations; friendly governments; the CIA; well-disguised racketeers trading in gambling; prostitution; even the occasional loan shark and extortionist. He had stayed away from drug dealers and revolutionaries. The latter were his enemies and had nothing to offer him anyway. Drug dealers were making headway into his department but until now he had resisted. Lopwitz, he knew, was not a drug dealer. 'Please continue.'

'Would you like an apartment in Miami?'

The offer sounded like a gift from heaven. The mortgage on the beachside *finca* he had bought two years ago with money accumulated from past bribes was absorbing much of his capital. His son and three daughters had not yet finished school. He had recently come to the reluctant realization that indulging his youthful fantasies of being a *haciendado*, a *hidalgo*, a member of the landed gentry, from when he was growing up as a poor boy in the Dominican slums, had been a mistake. That real estate in Florida would have been a far wiser investment.

The revolutionary tide that was sweeping through Central America threatened to convulse his own island nation. Despite the outward appearance of calm it was his duty to generate, Ventura had a foreboding that the years of tranquility and prosperity enjoyed since the Marines left in 1966 would soon come to an end. The ELD was gaining strength every day in the university and in the poor *barrios*. The violent demonstration of the other night could repeat itself at any time with far worse consequences. His men were not properly equipped for riot control. They did not even have tear gas. Bombings and assassinations were becoming more frequent. One of his subordinates had been shot in front of his home only a week ago and the next bullet could have his own name on it. His force was now scared to venture into certain parts of the city, refusing to patrol anywhere on foot. Three of his modest fleet of radio cars had been ambushed and burned.

He could soon find himself on the wrong side of the kind of civil war that had toppled Somoza in Nicaragua and was now raging in El Salvador. Or even more likely, there could be a military coup led by officers and politicians with whom he might find himself out of favor. There were already rumors. He would have nowhere to go, no place in which to hide, no sanctuary for his family. He kept eating.

'Are you interested in an apartment in Miami, Colonel, in return for doing a favor for me?' Lopwitz had to have Ventura's acceptance before he could go any further. 'It's in a luxury high-rise in Key Biscayne, a full view of the sea, four bedrooms, worth more than half a million dollars on the local market.' It was an apartment Lopwitz had bought when it was a project fifteen years ago. He had already made back his investment.

What could this fat Yankee want that could be worth all that? Certainly not bodyguards. Could he resist such an offer, even assuming Lopwitz were a drug dealer? 'Yes . . . I am interested . . . depends.'

Lopwitz needed to draw him a bit further in. 'As I told you, one of our people could get kidnapped here very soon.'

'And what do you want me to do?'

'Nothing.'

Lopwitz relaxed in the cocktail lounge of the Hotel Lima, enjoying a daquiri and a large Arturo Fuentes cigar. The kind they produced in the Dominican Republic were every bit as good as any Havana he had ever tasted.

It had been a good day's work. He had written out a three-month option on his Miami apartment for Ventura, giving him a set of keys and the name of the agency which handled it. Full ownership would be transferred in about a month if everything went well. Next, he had gone to a highly trusted local real estate agent recommended by Ventura.

'This will do,' Lopwitz had said the moment he took a look at the isolated villa hidden among the hills and rich tropical foliage just an hour's drive from the city. It had at one time been the main house of a sugar plantation. It was a bit rundown now but certainly habitable, with all the modern conveniences: full kitchen, color TV, a pool, a natural stream running just a few yards from the back of the house. The owner, who had lived in Florida for years, had even built a Jacuzzi.

'Can you connect CNN?'

'Yes, of course, Señor Weinstein.'

Lopwitz had handed the agent a three-month deposit.

There was still one thing left to do. He might have to stay over another night. Lopwitz had the last sip of his daquiri, took a few good puffs of his Arturo Fuentes and glanced around the darkened wood-paneled lounge, which had the atmosphere of a large humidor. The piano player in the far corner was playing the classic Latin love tune, *Sabor a Mi*. He suddenly caught sight of a striking-looking woman sitting alone at one of the tables. She wore a simple dark evening dress that clung to her every curve and gave full exposure to the cleavage for which Dominican women are famous. Her crossed legs and sleeveless arms were slender, but the rest of her had the voluptuousness of Sophia Loren. Long black hair hung over her shoulders, large brown eyes gleamed with little or no make-up and a full, sensually curved mouth gave the impression of unusual skill. Could she actually be . . . impossible, thought Lopwitz, she should be in Hollywood. He called over the bar tender, gesturing discreetly in her direction.

'*Viene aqui de vez en cuando, va con Senores. De muy alto categoria.*'

So she was. Lopwitz called over the waiter and told him to ask her if he could buy her a drink.

Following a brief exchange with the waiter, she nodded, looked in his direction and flashed an electrifying smile. She would appreciate a daquiri.

Lopwitz ordered two, walked over and introduced himself.

'My name is Nora,' came her ready reply.

When the drinks arrived, she picked up her daquiri and licked the crushed sugar around the rim of her glass with just the tip of her tongue, her eyes half closed in sensual enjoyment.

Lopwitz had not felt the heat of an instant erection in many years. But his body was aglow, his heart skipping beats and from his lower abdomen a rocket seemed to be blasting off. He felt like he could be eighteen again. Clearing his throat, he said, 'Do you usually come here?'

'Only when I have a date.' She glanced at her thin wristwatch. 'But I think I have been stood up.' Her face made a faint pout that was even better than her smile.

Lopwitz sure felt sorry for the husband who couldn't get away from his wife at the last moment.

She looked at Lopwitz, changing back into a smile. 'I could be some time with you if you like.' The tip of her tongue was licking the rim of her glass again.

A price was quickly fixed.

Once up in his suite, she just lifted the straps off her shoulders, letting the dress fall to the floor. She wore nothing underneath and took her place on the the bed. The nipples of her large hard breasts tilted upwards, her perfectly rounded bottom beckoned him and when he approached she unzipped his trousers and immediately went to work on his erection as her hands helped him to undress. Her moist vaginal odor was scented with a touch of expensive French perfume.

High-priced call girls he had been with before, even the best, could never seem to restrain a hint of disapproval of his slight obesity. Nora seemed oblivious to all except the long obesity protruding from below his stomach. As he lay down, she held it in the palm of her hand, rubbing it gently on her cheek and kissing it as she moaned softly, *'Hay Amor . . . lo tienes tan grande . . . Hayyyy mi boca . . . Hayy.'*

They relaxed in bed afterwards, drinking a bottle of champagne which he produced from the small refrigerator. She was so different from any other hooker he had ever been with. If she was a flawless actress, it didn't matter. She talked about wanting to go to the United States, but needing money and a visa. Her ambition was to get into the movies. She worked as a magazine model but despite the general promiscuousness of Santo Domingo, the Catholic censorship restricted the public expression of her attributes.

Lopwitz lit up an Arturo Fuentes. 'There is something more I may want you to do for me, Nora.' He handed her a pad and pen. 'Write down here how I can get in touch.'

John Clark kicked shut the bottom drawer of his chest. He took his neat pile of pressed cotton shirts and laid them out on top of his suitcase. He was going to go and stay in the Metropolitan Club. He had thought he could stick it out in his own home until his departure for Latin America but it had become unbearable in the two weeks since the elevator fight. Tiffany stood leaning with her back against the wall, arms crossed, trying to look concerned but emotionally indifferent.

'I mean it, Tiffany. When I get back from my trip I want this sordid affair of yours to be over or I'm filing for a divorce. That's final.'

She said nothing. She could not deny it any longer. She was in love with Julio and it wouldn't stop. In the days immediately following their big row she had tried to make things up with John. It came more easily after he told her that he was going off soon on a long business trip. She explained that she had stayed away that night at the house of an old schoolfriend because she was afraid of his bad temper. That she really had gone to consult about a modelling contract with a new agent whom Cruickshank did not know. Clark had tried to make himself believe that he believed her. But inside he knew. He had noticed her thinly concealed elation after he told her about the trip.

A conciliatory attempt at love-making proved to be a disaster. It was as if an invisible wall had come between them. She had stopped feeling any passion in her sex with John for well over a year. But this time it was John who couldn't manage it. He had burst into tears, saying that he felt like a castrated man. Her efforts to comfort him only made things worse. He slept in the spare bedroom after that night.

She had tried to cool things down with Julio, explaining, over his irresistible objections, that they would be able to see lots more of each other as soon as John left. But he wouldn't stop calling her and in the end she gave in and began to slip out to see him with increasing frequency.

Today John had returned early from the office to find the apartment empty. When she ran in the front door, half an hour later, he could see it, he could smell it.

She had forgotten to take along her make-up. Her dress was wrinkled, lipstick off, loose blonde hair tossed, the straps of her bra visible in her purse. She exuded the odor of fermented perfume. Her eyes were steamy.

'You've been with him again haven't you?'

'I've got nothing to say to you, John.'

'You are cheap.'

She ignored him and walked quickly to the master bedroom. He followed. 'You've turned into a cheap whore! . . . Tell me who the hell he is, goddamit!'

She couldn't control herself any longer. 'All I can say is that he is more man than you.'

He started packing. How he longed to make her feel sorry, to make her feel guilty. By the time Clark walked out of his apartment he needed to be a martyr. He actually hoped that something would happen to him on his Central American trip.

5

The Pan Am 747 approached the northern rim of the island of Hispaniola, divided roughly between Haiti on the western end and the Dominican Republic on the east. James Martin stared down into the green and turquoise calmness of the Caribbean.

He had gotten a leave of absence from Security International with no problem. His boss, Col Huckner, was very happy. He had been on the phone with Lopwitz, who was proposing that his site survey people have a look at some of Sanitex Equipment's plants in Pennsylvania. That's where the money was for Huckner. The terrorism information service that Martin ran was a useful sideshow to attract clients. It had worked and Martin was being heartily congratulated for bringing in a good one. Any notion he had of owning up to Huckner quickly vanished.

Suspicions that Lisa could be another ploy by Lopwitz to control his life were similarly ignored. His ego badly needed her blissful massaging. His experiences with Washington women over the years had frequently proved frustrating. He just could not bear to disentangle himself from her taut, tender body. She seemed even younger than twenty. Their lovemaking had been constant. He loved the way she pretended to resist him only to surrender with total gusto. She screamed during orgasms, sometimes moaning, 'I'm being raped,' then lapsing into giggles as they snuggled in post-coital happiness.

As far as he was concerned the job he had to do

was quite straightforward. In the unlikely event that Lopwitz had any hidden scheme in mind – what it could possibly be he could not venture a guess – it was not his responsibility. Or so he reassured himself.

Martin checked into the Hotel Lima where Lopwitz had reserved him a room paid one month in advance. It was already late evening. Between the flight and the humid heat, he was tired. After a dinner of sirloin steak washed down with ice-cold beer, he turned in for an early night. It was going to be a long day tomorrow.

His first stop in the morning was the police head-quarters. His taxi wound around the tree-lined streets of Santo Domingo's pleasant residential section. It passed through the spacious square in front of the baroque immensity of the presidential palace, built by Spanish viceroys. Martin noticed the platoon of guardsmen through the palace gates ceremonially uniformed in shocking-pink and plumed caps, drilling for a changing of the guard.

The exotic elegance of the scene contrasted sharply with the green concrete building where the taxi stopped, built like a fortress complete with parapets along the roof. A high wall topped by barbed wire extended out from the main building. Martin got out in front of sheet-metal gates where two police guards in olive drab fatigues and French-style blue képis stood inside the shade of wooden sentryboxes hunched over World War II M-1 rifles. One of them asked what his business was. Martin said he had an appointment to see Major Otero. The guard banged twice on the sheet metal with his rifle butt. The gates opened. A sergeant came out and gave a lackadaisical salute. He escorted him through the dusty courtyard, where more guards in olive fatigues and blue képis mingled around a jeep and a radio car, smoking and chatting. They climbed a long flight of steps to the entrance of the main building, past another wooden sentrybox.

It was like entering a dungeon after the blinding lash of the tropical sun. The daylight only came in rays through narrow barred windows. The fertilizer-like smell of cheap black tobacco clung in the moist air. Strip lighting flickered on and off down the narrow corridor leading to the offices of the intelligence department. The sergeant saluted Major Otero, who remained sitting with his boots on top of his desk, gesturing Martin towards the steel fold-out chair in front of him while his other hand waved a fly swatter.

Otero was a shade darker than the average Dominican mulatto. He had predatory eyes and an athletic chest. Not the man to face in an interrogation, and quite clearly not one who cared to be interrogated.

They had already talked by phone but Martin explained again the purpose of his visit. Otero replied that he never talked with outsiders but if the matter concerned security needs for a corporation, he would be willing to answer some questions, quickly adding that he knew of some excellent bodyguards. His fly swatter came down with a reverberating crash on top of a manilla folder. All that was left to see was a small splotch of blood. Otero scraped off the swatter over his trash can.

Martin explained that for the moment all he needed was an appraisal of subversive terrorist groups active in the Dominican Republic. Otero opened his drawer and fished out a list of five groups which his department was currently investigating, handing it to Martin.

The most serious threat, as Martin already knew, came from the one at the top of the list, Ejercito de Liberacion Dominicano (ELD). It was organized along Marxist-Leninist lines headed by a nine-member directorate, all of whom had at some point or other undergone guerrilla training in Cuba or had some association with the Castro régime. Its leader, Arturo Cayetano, known as *Comandante Nueve*, had spent three months at the Punto Cero military academy outside Havana. Recently the police had received information that one contingent of twenty to thirty men had gone to train with the Sandinistas in Nicaragua. They were expected to receive special instruction in demolitions and small-unit assault tactics, then to return to the Dominican Republic for an intensified phase of terrorist attacks against the government.

The ELD tested its recruits in street battles with police like the one which took place in front of the new opera house last week. Those who made the best account of themselves were chosen for more advanced training. The organization was active throughout the country with guerrilla '*focos*' in rural parts of the interior and highly active cells dispersed around Santo Domingo. *Comandante Nueve* was known to favor an urban over a rural strategy. The ELD already exercised considerable control over certain areas of the *barriadas* or slums which ringed the capital. It was credited with the recent killing of Otero's deputy commander of intelligence, Capitan Ruiz, who was shot in the back from a passing car as he returned home from work one evening. Otero went over a series of other incidents attributed to the ELD including a recent car bombing outside the offices of IBM. Equipped with arms from Cuba, it had sufficient capability to stage an important kidnapping in Otero's opinion. Bang! Another fly. The Major moved his swatter with the swiftness of a karate chop.

He went further down the list in a dispassionate manner, as if he were describing items on a shopping list. The Grupo Armado Revolucionario (GAR) was a splinter faction of the ELD, not as large, but armed with automatic weapons and some explosives. It had carried out numerous attacks on police and a recent machine-gun strafing of the American Consulate. The other groups on the list, Cuerpo Comunista Primero de Octubre (CCIO), Estudiantes y Trabajadores para la Liberacion (ETPL) and Organizacion Tercerista Insurreccional (OTI), were mainly student-based, explained Otero. Their members had participated in various street confrontations with the police. He did not, however, believe that they possessed any significant organization or armed strength.

Martin took notes and asked the Major if there was a potential for any new groups to develop.

'*Si, claro que hay esa posibilidad.*' Another fly buzzed past his head. He looked around abruptly, lifting the swatter. 'There is one *grupo, por ejemplo* . . . we have not looked into it yet.' The fly would not land. Otero's eyes followed it. '*Mierda, esa maldita mosca.*'

'What's the name of that group, just for my record?'

The fly landed just on the tip of Otero's knee; his eyes fully fixed on it, he lifted the swatter slowly. 'Fart' . . . it came down to score a direct hit again. Otero flicked off the miniature carcass with his fingernail.

Martin was surprised to hear the Major swear in English. 'What's the name of the group, Major Otero?'

'I told you, FART, Frente Armado Revolucionario de Trabajadores.'

Martin finally realized that the acronym did not mean anything in Spanish.

'They held up a McDonald's hamburger restaurant the other night, taking money and some hamburgers while their leader, this *Comandante* Carlos, gave a speech to the attendants and customers about supporting the revolution. They handed out printed literature about their group and spray-painted 'FART' all over the McDonald's sign outside. *Solo seran unos gamberros haciendose pasar por revolucionarios.* We can't take them too seriously. We have enough on our hands.' His eyes focused on another fly.

Martin returned to the hotel for lunch, his shirt soaked through with perspiration. He changed into a pair of bathing trunks and went to the pool for a swim. He dried in the burning sun and ate a sandwich at the snack bar. The *café-au-lait* beauties gyrated around him, but he could not afford to get distracted. The outline Otero had given him on terrorist organizations in Santo Domingo was a start. But now came the difficult part of actually getting in to talk with some of these groups. Before leaving Washington, Martin had indirectly contacted the National Office of Latin America, a leading lobby for leftist causes, obtaining the number of a legal aid office in Santo Domingo which gave various types of assistance to the revolutionary underground. On the phone to them this morning he had explained that he was a journalist and now he expected a call back.

Martin was in his room changing into a pair of jeans, sneakers and a safari shirt when the phone rang. Somebody called Octavio was on the line, telling him to be at an anti-government demonstration that was planned for that afternoon in the Plaza de la Catedral. He should go to the speaker's platform which would be on an open truck and ask for him.

The taxi dropped Martin off about two blocks from the plaza, on one of the side-streets. Police and army troops were closing off the area to traffic although not interfering with the rally itself, which Martin could see was in full progress with a crowd of about two thousand gathered in front of the old gothic cathedral. They were cheering a man who spoke emotionally through a bullhorn from the top of the open truck. Red banners, announcing the presence of many of the groups Otero had told him about, were everywhere. Evidence of support for the ELD among the mostly young participants was strong. Many of them wore the red and black bandanas of the guerrilla movement. As he walked into the open square, Martin could hear the speaker more clearly shouting about how they were gathered to 'mark the tenth day since the killing of our *compañeros* before the very eyes of President

Camuñas by the murderous forces of the régime . . . the time has come for all of our Dominican brothers and sisters to rise up against the forces of imperialism and oppression. The blood spilled by our *compañeros* is the baptism of our revolution . . . *Revolucion o Muerte, Viva la Revolucion!*'

'*Viva la Revolucion!*' came the enthusiastic response from the multitude, followed by chanting of '*El Pueblo Unido jamas sera Vencido. El Pueblo Unido jamas sera Vencido* . . .'

Martin decided to walk around the crowd instead of through it to get to the platform truck where Octavio would be waiting. He noticed three jeeps unloading helmeted police armed with batons and rifles to block access to an avenue leading from the square with offices of some important foreign banks. Another speaker was now having his turn at the bullhorn. Martin kept on walking. He was right at the back of the crowd as a steady stream of demonstrators arrived to thicken it. Most of them wore the red and black bandanas, some using them to cover their faces. Some were shirtless. He moved with more difficulty now towards the main street, bypassing the square as another jeep arrived to unload more helmeted figures in olive drab to cordon off the avenue. A group of about twenty youngsters, gathered around a red cloth banner with the initials E.L.D. stitched on it in white, blocked his view as he heard a far-off crackling noise, like loud fireworks. There was confusion. Then again, more crackling, louder this time. There was no doubt about it, it was gunfire. The crowd started heaving in all directions, a chain reaction of shouting and screams. The speaker's words were drowned out although he continued standing on top of the truck. Now hollower blasts of heavier caliber arms returning fire, from the direction of the military jeeps, echoed around the square.

Martin started moving with the human tide away

from the cathedral. More light firing now came from somewhere near him and then the deafening thunder of a rifle volley. People were running in all directions, many falling over each other as police charged in from the side-streets. He could see some blood-drenched bodies amidst the human whirlpool being helped up or dragged by friends. There was more rifle fire, coming nearer this time. Martin dove for cover behind a stone bench. He lay there snuggled between the ground and the protective stone block. Others were joining him. He sensed a flying shadow over the stone bench above him. The body landed heavily on his back.

'Ouch!'

'*Perdoneme.*' A youngish fit-looking man in a loose shirt with a black beard frantically made room for himself next to Martin. Dispersing demonstrators kept running past him, gunfire still reverberating around the square. 'What is your name?'

'Martin.'

'*Extranjero?*'

'*Americano.*' Martin hastened to add, 'Journalist.'

'Ah, *periodista*,' came the approving rejoinder. A bullet ricocheted off the stone bench.

'You are covering the rally, no? Now you can tell your readers in America about the truth of what is happening in the Dominican Republic. *Estos Asesinos!*'

Martin could hardly speak, but the words just came out. 'I'm writing an article about revolutionary groups here.'

'*Hay que suerte.* I have a revolutionary group.'

'What do you mean, you have a revolutionary group?' Another bullet ricocheted nearby, but the apparent nonchalance of his new companion towards the disintegrating universe around them actually gave Martin a peculiar feeling of reassurance.

'I am the leader.'

'Of what?'

'The FART.'

'The FART!'

'*Frente Armado Revolucionario de Trabajadores.*'

The Armed Workers' Revolutionary Front. It was the group which had robbed the McDonald's, the one which Major Otero was not bothering to investigate.

'Would you like to do an article on my organization?'

'If we ever get out of here.' The gunfire was very close now. Martin saw a shirtless youth in jeans with a red and black bandana covering his face standing behind a tree. He had just finished loading his revolver and was taking aim at some target in front of him, undoubtedly at the police. He fired a shot and ran off. Several rifle rounds whizzed in his direction.

Martin could hear the thud of heavy boots approaching. Soon a pair was by his face and the next moment one was into his ribs. He felt himself getting picked up by the arm and neck, with the cold numbing sensation of a gun barrel pressed against his head as he was searched. They were doing the same with the leader of FART. Martin gave a silent prayer. If his newfound acquaintance was carrying a gun they would probably both get shot on the spot with no questions asked. Fortunately there was no gun. The relief was enough for him momentarily to forget the sharp pain from where he had been kicked in his left ribcage.

'*Que hacen ustedes aqui?*' barked the helmeted sergeant.

Martin got the words out: '*Soy Americano, periodista.*' Then he had another idea. 'I know Major Otero, spoke with him this morning.'

His eyes could now focus on the man, who was demanding his passport. Martin gestured towards his breast pocket where his passport was with a fifty-dollar bill folded inside. The sergeant pulled it out. He glanced at it and walked a few yards, saluting a superior who also took a look. Four soldiers – or police, it was not really possible to distinguish between the two in the Dominican Republic once they were helmeted – continued to point their rifles at them. The sergeant came back, handing over the passport – minus the fifty dollars. '*Con que conoze al Mayor Otero?*'

'*Si, tuvimos una entrevista esta manana.*'

'*Vayase. Pero detengan a este otro.*' The sergeant pointed at the leader of FART.

Martin thought he would chance it. Otero, after all, had said they did not know who the members of FART were. 'He is my guide, *es mi guia,*' Martin explained.

'*Es su guia?*'

'*Si,* he brought me to this demonstration so I could see how the forces of order are provoked by extremists.'

The sergeant hesitated. '*Ya, vayanse los dos.* But abandon the plaza immediately.'

Martin and the leader of FART were escorted out through the debris of the Plaza de la Catedral. At least twenty to thirty wounded and dying bodies lay about unattended. Shots still rang out from one of the side-streets where a group of demonstrators had barricaded themselves for a pitched battle with police and troops. Scores of people were being lined up with their hands behind their heads by rifle-toting guardsmen. Army trucks were now pulling into the plaza to haul them off to detention.

Once safely inside a taxi, the leader of FART introduced himself as Carlos, thanking Martin profusely for saving him from getting arrested. He offered to take him for a drink to '*un local muy bueno donde hay muchas chicas.*' Martin accepted.

Darkness was falling as the taxi stopped in front of the entrance to a private-looking house walled off from a pot-holed street with otherwise cheap-looking wooden row houses. No sooner had they walked through the small garden and taken their places at a table in the porch of 'Casa Las Familias', than they were surrounded by eagerly solicitous young girls, mostly in their teens. Some of them displayed their plump breasts while others lifted their thin dresses, offering it all. Carlos gestured with two fingers at the waiter who promptly arrived with a bottle of rum, ice bucket, and two bottles of Coca-Cola. The girls, Carlos explained, were not pros, but 'son chicas de por aqui – who live with their families or have other jobs and come here to have fun and make an extra buck.' Prostitution was casual and more or less accepted in Santo Domingo. There were rooms at the back of the house. The girls had to have a weekly medical checkup to come here. The doctor was paid by the house and Carlos, a former medical student, assisted him. His girls got their checkups at reduced rates.

Despite his enthusiasm for subsidized medicine, Carlos was hardly what Martin would consider to be a dedicated Marxist. Still, since he was ingratiated with the leader of FART, he might as well have a look at the group. They could have other connections, and he would have something to tell Lopwitz, who would call for a progress report in the next few days. It would probably be difficult to re-establish contact with the people he was supposed to meet at the rally that afternoon. Carlos had told him during their taxi ride that martial law would undoubtedly be declared now. Everyone would be lying very low.

'Let me take you up on your offer to have me write an article about your group.' Martin half-emptied his glass of rum and Coke.

'How do I know you are not CIA; you said in the plaza that you spoke with Major . . .'

'Hay es de la Cia!' An astounded chorus went up from their fan club. A prettier, much older girl broke her way through them. She pulled up a chair next to Martin, unbuttoning her blouse.

'You just have to trust me.' It was becoming very difficult to concentrate as she ran her fingers up his thigh. 'I saved you from getting arrested didn't I? Besides, what kind of a place is this to say that? *You* can't be too professional, Carlos.'

The girl's hand was on his chest now, and she was cooing in his ear. '*Hay amor comprame una copa, dame veinte dollares para hacer el amor contigo . . . por favor.*' She licked his earlobe.

'They are all *compañeras*. They do not repeat anything I don't want.'

'You must have a large group.'

'What do you want to know?'

'I would like to . . . is this any kind of place to carry on an interview?' Martin had an annoyed tone.

Carlos downed the last of the rum and Coke in his glass. 'Wait here. Take Graciela on me. I will come back in an hour.'

By the time Martin was walking back out of the bedroom, with Graciela smiling beside him as she did up her blouse, Carlos was waiting.

'I take you to interview the full executive committee of my organization. There is a car outside. But you have to come blindfolded, *amigo*. We take it off when you are in our headquarters.'

He got into the back seat with Carlos and another person who tied the blindfold around his eyes. The car drove around the backstreets of Santo Domingo for what seemed like an eternity. He then felt himself dizzily being led out and into a house, past several rooms and then down a flight of steps. When the blindfold came off, he was in a dugout basement which served as the headquarters of the *Frente Armado Revolucionario de Trabajadores*. The initials F.A.R.T. were stitched in white on a red cloth which hung pegged to the dirt wall. The room was illuminated by a naked light bulb that hung from the low ceiling. Carlos and four others wearing balaclavas took their place in rickety chairs around the table which were the only furniture. Martin also noticed some boxes containing various papers, some small-caliber ammunition and a few sticks of dynamite. Carlos introduced the hooded members of his executive committee by numbers *dos*, *tres*, *cuatro* and *cinco*.

'First we need to ask you some questions, *amigo*.' It was Carlos. 'What did you talk about with Major Otero?'

'As I told you, I'm preparing an article about the revolutionary movement in your country. I interviewed Major Otero the same way I am interviewing you now.'

'Did he say anything about us?'

'He just mentioned your group in passing.'

'What did he actually say, *Señor* Martin?' Carlos was being insistent.

'I don't remember quite well. He said something about you robbing a McDonald's stand and scrawling your initials on the sign outside.'

'What else did he say?'

'That's all. As I've told you, I don't remember that well.'

'He must have said something else, *Señor* Martin. You spoke to him this morning you say?'

'Hey, I'm the one who should be asking questions here.' Martin was getting impatient.

'Before we answer any of your questions we want to know everything that Major Otero said about us.'

'Well, he said . . . he said that you are just a bunch of delinquents and he doesn't take your group seriously. He is not bothering to investigate you. You are not on his list of dangerous groups if that is any comfort.'

There was some murmuring around the table. Carlos looked clearly upset. 'That's what he said about us?! *Carajo, ese hijo de puta.*' He ran his hand around his face in nervous embarrassment. 'First those other *hijos de puta* in the ELD tell the Cubans not to have anything to do with us and now that *negro cabron* slanders us in front of the press.'

Carlos picked up a bottle of rum from the floor and took a large gulp then passed it around the table. It came around to Martin, who also took a gulp.

'You know, *Señor* Martin, we tried to join the ELD some months ago. But they said that we are not disciplined revolutionaries. After I told them that I disagreed with their tactic of provoking police to shoot at demonstrators causing innocent people to be killed, the leader of ELD, that cruel, mean *hijo de puta Comandante Nueve*, gave the order to cut off any contact with us. He would not help to arrange for us to go to Cuba to train as *guerrilleros*. We tried to approach directly the Cuban agent here who works as bureau chief of the *Prensa Latina*, the Cuban news agency. But he refused to talk to us. So we decided to form our own revolutionary movement.'

'So now you rob McDonald's stands?'

'It was an act of revolutionary expropriation from Yankee multi-national capitalists that are sucking the blood of our country . . . we needed the money, *amigo* . . . to buy arms.' He pointed towards the boxes with the dynamite and ammunition. 'Our strategy is to strike at the heart of the system of oppression. We don't want to shed any innocent blood. Our next act is going to be an important step in the liberation of the Republica Dominicana.' All those around the table nodded in agreement.

'What is this next act of yours going to be?'

'Ah, that we cannot say. At the moment we are preparing and gathering our strength . . . according to the prescriptions of Lenin.'

'You were a medical student before becoming a revolutionary, right, Carlos?'

'That's right. My father was paying for my studies. He has a small hacienda in the north of the country near Puerto Plata. But now I'm dedicated to fighting for socialism. I also have . . . well, I also have my women, *amigo*.'

Martin asked the rest of the group what they did.

Dos: 'I was also studying medicine. But now I'm a dedicated revolutionary like our leader.'

Tres: 'I've had many jobs driving delivery trucks.'

Cuatro: 'I work in an accounting office. I wanted to go to America to work a year ago. But I couldn't get a visa.'

Cinco, who Martin now noticed was a woman: 'I worked in a restaurant, then a beauty shop and then for Carlos. I also could not get a visa to America. Now, I'm a dedicated revolutionary.'

'What's the total number in your group?'

'We are the core cell,' replied Carlos, 'but our supporters could be fifty or sixty.'

There was general agreement around the table with murmurs of '*muchos . . . muchos*.'

'Don't you want to take any photographs of us, *amigo*?' It was Carlos. 'With hoods on naturally, underneath our banner?'

'Well, I don't have my camera.'

Carlos's face lit up. 'I have idea. Come with us tomorrow. We go for target practice in *el campo*. You can take pictures of us shooting, preparing for the revolution. What you say?' Carlos gave Martin a strong slap on the back; he held in the pain, though his ribs still hurt and he realized that he also had a sunburn. '*Que dicen todos*, eh?' Carlos asked the group.

There were some murmurs, but finally, they all agreed.

6

Martin was waking up late on his third morning in Santo Domingo. He had had serious second thoughts about wasting any more time with Carlos, but had finally decided over breakfast, the previous day, to make his arranged rendezvous and accompanied the FART to their target practice session. He had been driven – blindfolded again the last stretch of the way – to an abandoned farmhouse about an hour from the city. The FART had their entire arsenal, consisting of two old ·38 caliber revolvers, one Colt ·45 automatic pistol and a sawn-off shotgun. It had been the most pathetic display of marksmanship he had ever seen. They shot their pistols like in the old Western movies, aiming them from their sides with one hand instead of holding them directly in front with both. He had to restrain himself from telling them how combat firing was really done, not wanting to suddenly be transformed into a weapons adviser to a budding group of terrorists.

Some of the girls from Las Familias joined them later, bringing a picnic of roast pork sandwiches, fruit and wine. Graciela had come with them. She was now stretched horizontally across his hotel bed giving an enthusiastic treatment to his morning's erection.

Never had he seen a woman go at it with such total devotion and such a fine rhythm. First wrapping her tongue around for a few strokes, then inside her mouth, bringing it up, bringing it up, bringing it up, then just the tongue again. Then, her lips and tongue just around the tip, then stroking it gently with her hand as she looked up hungrily for the approving moan. Then the tongue around all of it, then all the way into her mouth. And then, and then the phone rang on his night table. He picked it up. It was Lopwitz calling from New York. 'Hello, Martin, how are you getting on?'

'Oh, fine, Herb, just fine. How are you?'

'I'm sure you've got warmer weather down there.'

'We sure do.'

'So, what have you got for me?'

'Well, Herb, I spoke with the head of police intelligence who gave me a rundown on all the groups which pose a terrorist threat down here.'

Graciela, who did not speak any English, bounced off the bed towards the bathroom, those beautiful breasts and buttocks moving in perfect harmony. Her soft skin was a very light coffee color. There was a natural loveliness in her face.

'Have you actually managed to establish contact with any of them?'

'Oh, that I have. I went to this demonstration two days ago to meet with someone who was supposed to take me around. It turned into a total riot, gun-battle is more like it. Almost got myself killed. Got roughed up a bit.'

'Oh yeah, read about it. Be careful. Hope you're all right?'

'Yeah, I'm fine. Anyway, I lost contact with him and the only number I've got didn't answer all of yesterday. Martial law has been declared. All of the opposition are lying very low. But through another source, I've managed to speak to the leader of another, of . . . a small group.'

'What's it called?'

'Are you ready for this, Herb? The FART.'

'The what?'

'FART.' Martin broke into laughter.

'Is this some kind of a joke?' Lopwitz almost seemed annoyed.

'It might as well be. But it is actually a group that exists here. The initials stand for Workers' Armed Revolutionary Front.'

'But that's WART, no, sorry, WARF.'

'But in Spanish it's FART.'

'So what can you tell me about them?'

'They just seem to be a bunch of confused guys. They talk about going to Miami one moment and about the revolution the next. Their leader is some kind of a pimp. I spoke to them at their safe house. The only revolutionary act they've done so far was to hold up a McDonald's. They spray-painted FART all over where it says More than thirty million sold . . . The Police Intelligence chief had mentioned the group as an afterthought. He's not even bothering to investigate it. Nobody takes them seriously. Even according to their own leader, this Carlos, the other guerrilla groups here don't want anything to do with them . . .'

Lopwitz seemed all ears. 'Continue.'

'Okay, this guy, Carlos, he claims that they are planning some big action which will put them at the forefront of the revolutionary movement. What that could be I can't possibly imagine.' Martin erupted into more laughter. 'I went out with them to their target practice yesterday. They have a couple of rusty thirty-eights. I'm not sure that they could hit a standing target a foot in front of them.'

'You've done a good job, Martin. I'll be down in a couple of days. Stay right where you are.'

Graciela was bouncing back on the bed with an eager smile on her face. Martin was only too glad to follow Lopwitz's instructions.

For the next two days he did not venture out of the hotel. Graciela stayed with him the whole time, either in his bed or down by the pool. He bought her an orange tanga bikini at the hotel's boutique. It fitted her young body like a ribbon around a Christmas present. When they were not making love or watching the CNN channel – switching occasionally to the local news to get the latest on the political situation as martial law went into effect and images came through of military vehicles rolling around Santo Domingo – they lay talking. She told him of how bored she was. How she was planning to enter university next year, but did not know what to study. There were no worthwhile jobs to be had. She had not found any man she wished to marry and she wanted to go to America, but was not sure she could get a visa.

Graciela told him that she went to Las Familias occasionally to pick up some money. But she chose her own customers. If she did not like a man she would not go to bed with him. She assured Martin that she no longer considered him a customer. She would accept presents from him, but no payments.

When he asked her about Carlos, she said she liked him but thought that his group was a joke. She was scared by the idea of a revolution anyway and hated the ELD. Her father owned several shops and had already been approached by guerrillas demanding regular protection payments.

She laughed incessantly when Martin told her what FART meant in English. Carlos should never know, she said, he was so proud of his group. She spoke about how he was such a wild man. He had assaulted a policeman once, knocking him unconscious from the back and stealing his revolver . . . 'Ese no es mas marxista que yo, es un aventurero.' She worried that he would eventually get arrested and it would be the end of FART. 'Now I can't stop laughing every time I say that name.'

Martin had just come back up from the pool with Graciela on the third afternoon of his Dominican romance, looking forward to an active nap, when the phone rang. It was Lopwitz. He had just gotten in from New York and was checking into his suite two floors above. Would Martin come up to meet with him in about an hour, room 510. He had time for at least one good go with Graciela, who had just skipped out of her tanga.

Lopwitz had left the door open. 'Would you close the door behind you, Martin. Please sit down; have a drink.' He gestured towards the empty swivel chair opposite him. There was a bottle of Scotch, an ice bucket and two glasses on the table. Martin poured himself one on the rocks as Lopwitz prepared his pipe.

He gave it the first hard puffs. 'First off, Martin, let me congratulate you on an excellent job done so far.'

'Excellent? I've only gotten into one small group and they are not a threat to anybody, unless you happen to eat at McDonald's.'

They both laughed.

'Well, Martin, that's the point, that's exactly the group I'm looking for. You could not have hit on a better one if you had researched up and down Santo Domingo for a year.'

'I don't think I understand what you mean.' Martin sipped his Scotch. The foreboding feeling he had had about Lopwitz during their last meeting at the Cosmos Club in Washington was coming back all over again.

'Martin.' Lopwitz puffed steadily at his pipe. 'Now comes the real part of what I've brought you down here to do for me.'

Martin drank more of his Scotch.

'From what you have told me this terrorist group FART sounds perfect for what I have in mind. I want you to prepare it to stage a kidnapping for me in the next couple of weeks.'

'What? I don't think that I understand you correctly, Mr Lopwitz.'

'I know this may sound incredible to you, Martin,

but just reserve any further comment until you hear fully what I have to say, then we can discuss it.'

'Discuss it! Herb, if you have said what I think you have just said, you are asking me to lead a terrorist kidnapping. Are you out of your mind?'

'Martin, please let me talk.'

Martin took another large gulp of his Scotch, feeling as if he were entering a bad dream.

'I have taken out a K & R insurance policy of twenty-four and a half million dollars on one of our Vice Presidents who is expected here in about two weeks. My plan is to stage a bogus kidnapping using a group with some terrorist track record as a front and collect the ransom insurance so that I may use it as a discretionary fund to rescue the Sanitex Equipment Corporation from bankruptcy. Have I made myself clear? It is really quite simple.'

'You are out of your mind, Herb.'

'Quite the contrary, Martin. I'm very sane. It is you who will lose your mind if you do not follow along with my plans. If you do, I will make you a rich man.'

'Herb, what you are asking me to do is . . .'

'What I am asking you to do is the culmination of what you have been doing for the past five years or however long you have been with Security International. You have scientifically exposed predictable methods and patterns of terrorist operations. I am now giving you an opportunity to put your knowledge into practice by managing a terrorist operation from which you stand to gain great personal benefit.'

Martin was about to interrupt but Lopwitz sat up in his chair looking directly into his eyes. 'You are a young man and a virile man. Do you honestly envisage wasting away the rest of your life in an attic with a computer? Writing reports that hardly anyone reads? Living from hand to mouth? Chasing women that don't give you the time of day because you do not have the money that you should have? All for a few brief moments of glory at lecture meetings and the occasional passing reference in the *New York Times*. I've talked to the CIA about you and they think you are a loser. Don't you honestly think that you deserve better than that?'

'But what you are asking me to do is to commit a fraud, Herb, criminal fraud. A kidnapping! I could end up in some jail down here. If their jails are anything like the police headquarters, I would rather be in the Black Hole of Calcutta!'

'Don't worry about going to jail, if you are working for me the police here won't touch you. It's been arranged.' Lopwitz relit his pipe. 'As for the fraud . . .' he puffed a bit '. . . what's it actually to you if the biggest insurance company in the world writes off a few peanuts in a payment which as far as they are concerned is part of their business and perfectly legitimate anyway? Just worry about yourself, Martin, I assure you that Lloyds of London will survive.'

'But I've got contacts there. If Ian ever . . .'

'What contacts, Martin? When I mentioned your name to Ian Whitecliff he hardly even remembered who the hell you were. Don't give yourself any false importance, my boy, you are just a young guy trying to make it and I'm giving you the chance to make something of yourself. Now, you are going to do this for me, aren't you?'

Herb Lopwitz was making it sound as if turning down his preposterous proposal would be like refusing an invitation to the royal wedding because you had to clean out your basement that afternoon. Martin fought hard inside against having his world turned upside down but was finding it as difficult as standing on a capsizing boat. He washed down the last of his Scotch, placed the glass firmly back on the table and stood up. 'Thanks for the drink, Herb, I'm walking out of here right now. As far as I'm concerned this conversation has not taken place. I'm catching the next plane to Miami.'

'If they let you out of the country, that is.' Lopwitz kept puffing at his pipe.

Martin's motion slowed. He was incredulous.

'I told you I had things arranged with the police, didn't I? You are a dangerous terrorist, Martin. There's martial law. You have been consorting with a violent subversive group. You lied to prevent one of their leaders from getting arrested a few days ago. You are not a journalist. Nobody knows that you are here working for me, except me.'

It took Martin all of his strength to stand up. 'I spoke with the head of police intelligence . . .'

'And a week ago I spoke to the people who tell the head of police intelligence what to do. If FART was not on their list of terrorist groups before, it is now.'

Martin felt like an animal being roped in. 'Why, you sonova . . .'

'Get it off your chest if you like, Martin. But please sit back down and have another drink. You are going to need one. I want you to hear something.' Lopwitz reached for the briefcase that was beside him, placing it on his lap. 'Security International, by the way, is right now in the process of entering into a merger deal with a firm to which I have introduced your boss Huckner. They are offering a pretty good price and he is very pleased. I've talked to him about giving you a good chunk if it goes through. You see, Martin, I will look after your interests if you play your cards right and come through for me. Otherwise, I hardly think that Huckner is going to be too happy if the apple-cart gets upset by a dishonest employee who works with terrorists behind his back and pays checks he has earned on the company's time into his own personal account.' Lopwitz casually produced a copy of the cancelled five-hundred-dollar check he had signed for his consultancy the morning in which they first met. Martin flopped back down into his seat, a look of horror sweeping over his face.

Lopwitz poured him a good helping of Scotch, throwing in a couple of ice cubes. 'Don't take it personally, Martin. Nobody's perfect. Including you. Everybody has their weaknesses and yours is between your legs.' He had now fished out a small tape recorder which he placed on the table. He snapped in a minicassette. 'You are now going to hear what else awaits you if you upset my plans, if you walk out on me or double-cross me in any way. This is a rape scene.' Lopwitz turned on the cassette.

It was Lisa's voice. 'Oh, don't, don't!'

Martin's heavy breathing. 'Come on baby, you love it, you know you love it.' The noise of clothes being forcefully taken off.

Lisa's voice: 'Oh, I'm being raped! I'm being raped! A terrorist! . . . Ahhh!'

'You love it, babe, you just love it.'

'Don't!' Another scream.

'Heard enough?' He switched it off. 'Or should I play some more? It's well edited.'

Martin was in shock. His red sunburn paled. Cold sweat formed on his brow.

'I've left a copy of this tape with certain attorneys in Washington. One phone call from me and a warrant will be issued for your arrest within hours. You see, even if you escape going to jail here, you will end up in a jail in DC. They are not much better.'

There was no resistance left in Martin. He croaked, 'She would never . . .'

'Are you sure she wouldn't, Martin? You knew her for about a week. I've known her for years. I've been putting her through school since her father died of a heart attack after losing a fortune in the stock market. I'm like her guardian. You see, I own the apartment in which you *raped* Lisa. The tape is not actually even necessary, although it does add some drama. Lisa didn't tell you. She is going to be eighteen next month. You just missed her age of consent. The rape is statutory. She does not even have to press charges. I can, especially since it took place on my property. I have great plans for Lisa. She wants to become an actress.' Lopwitz paused. Martin said nothing. After puffing his pipe a bit, he continued. 'You will be arraigned on rape charges. There will be no one to bail you out. And while a lot of mean, big, black criminals in Lorton prison are getting to know you, the government of the Dominican Republic will be demanding your extradition on charges of terrorist conspiracy. The press will love it: *Georgetown Girl Raped by Terrorist.*'

Martin was feeling acutely nauseous; his whole world was being turned upside down.

'You'd better face the fact that there is no escape, Martin. I've had weeks to prepare and you are caught entirely by surprise. I can go on and tell you more about what your life, or what's left of it, will become if you try to run. But I think you've got the picture. If you do what you're told, on the other hand, you will be perfectly safe. More than safe. You will make a lot of money. You will be secure. You will have as much or as many Lisas as you like. You won't find yourself in this situation again, that's for sure. Innocence is like virginity, Martin, you can only lose it once and when you do is when you really start living.'

Martin just let go, he felt enormously better. 'What if the insurance company doesn't pay the ransom? What if they find out it's a fraud in some way?'

'That's a risk we all have to take. But from the extended conversations I had with Whitecliff, I don't see how we can fail. You remain here in Santo Domingo managing the kidnapping from behind the scenes. Follow my directions, applying your knowledge about terrorism and your communications skills to make the threat appear real. It will be your skills

71

matched up against those of the ransom negotiators. You are in the big league now, Martin. I expect you to play like a pro. When the ransom is paid, I will let you arrange a cut for yourself of about half a million dollars, another half million for the FART. I have to clear at least twenty million for us to settle. If I'm satisfied with your performance, I will see to it that you get your job back and are provided for regardless of the outcome. Is it a deal?'

It was an offer Martin could not refuse, especially the half million dollars. His objections were now technical. 'But we need to train these guys. I told you, they can't even shoot straight. We need to set up a safe house or a network of them ... I'm not sure two weeks is enough ... Herb, what if something happens to this Vice President of yours?'

'Nothing will happen to him, I assure you. It's in nobody's interest, least of all FART's. I will personally see to it that he is well taken care of. The safe house has already been arranged. If these guys can just drive a car and *hold* a gun straight, that's all that should be required of them. You may have to work on the leader of the group a little bit, he may at some point have to meet directly with the negotiators, although that should be avoided. You will need someone reliable to run messages. We will also need a doctor or someone with medical experience to administer tranquilizers during initial stages of the kidnapping.'

Martin was now the accomplice. 'The leader of FART, Carlos, and another member of the group were medical students.'

'There you go, perfect. I'm telling you, Martin, you have found the perfect guys to do this.'

'What if they refuse to go along?'

'If they don't go along we can have them all busted. But we shouldn't need to threaten them. You yourself say that they are not serious Communists. That they all want to go to Miami. That they are just a bunch of frustrated guys trying to make something out of the revolution. That their leader is a pimp. Do you think that they are going to turn down a serious opportunity to make one hundred thousand dollars each? These guys have less to hang on to than you, Martin, they don't even get quoted in the *New York Times*.'

Martin now found himself again in the dugout basement headquarters before the full executive committee of the FART, illuminated by a naked light bulb hanging from the ceiling. When he got back to his room from his talk with Lopwitz the previous evening, he had pressed some money into Graciela's hand over her objections, kissed her goodnight and asked her to set up a meeting between him and Carlos as soon as possible.

'Carlos, would you please ask them to take off their hoods. I managed to see their faces the other day anyway, now will you please ask them to take those goddam things off.'

'It's revolutionary formality, *amigo*.'

'To hell with revolutionary formality, Carlos, if I'm going to propose something important to all of you, I want to see everyone's face.'

Carlos had insisted that he would only discuss business in front of his entire committee. '*Quitense las capuchas, el periodista solo nos propondra lo que tiene que proponernos si nos la quitamos.*' There were some nervous protests, but one by one they all started coming off. When *Cinco* took hers off, Martin could see why she had once worked for Carlos.

Martin thought he would start out by appealing to their revolutionary pride. 'What I want to propose to you may strike some of you as rather unorthodox, but as it says in the *Minimanual for the Urban Guerrilla* written by your famous namesake –' he turned briefly to Carlos ' – the Brazilian guerrilla leader Carlos

Marighuela, "adaptability is the key to a good revolutionary". Your movement could have a great significance for the revolutionary development of your country. That is why I have decided to try to enlist your cooperation.' He could hear *Cinco* and *Cuatro* murmuring between themselves about the CIA but they continued listening attentively.

Martin cleared his throat. 'I can turn you overnight from a small, struggling although dedicated band of *guerrilleros* into an important movement at the vanguard of the revolution in your country. You would have money, recognition, fame, anything that a . . . revolutionary movement could want.'

'And what do we have to do for all this, *amigo*?' It was Carlos who sat beside him.

Martin was slightly nervous now. 'What you have to do, Carlos, is just do what you told me that you were going to do when I interviewed you here last time: commit a very important revolutionary act. Except that now, I can help you. I can provide you with all the facilities, advice and protection you need. What I want you and your group to do –' Martin cleared his throat again '– is to stage a kidnapping.'

Loud voices this time all around the table. Carlos maintained an incredulous silence. Then: 'You want us to do a kidnapping, *amigo*?'

'That's quite correct, Carlos, but it's a, well, a special type of kidnapping and you have to agree to certain conditions.'

'Who do you really work for, *amigo*?'

'Well, you see, Carlos, I really am a journalist, a freelance journalist, but I've been hired to manage this kidnapping by the company of the person who you are supposed to kidnap.'

'You have been hired to kidnap someone by the company of the person who is going to be kidnapped. I don't understand, *amigo*.'

'I didn't think you would, Carlos, let me explain

myself a bit further. You see, this company has taken out insurance. Do you understand insurance?' Carlos nodded. 'Right, it has taken out insurance against kidnapping on one of its executives. That is, a policy which guarantees that a certain ransom will be paid in the event that he is kidnapped. Do you understand me so far?'

Most around the table nodded in silence.

'Now, what we want to do is physically execute the kidnapping, claiming it in the name of FART. I will tell you who and when. After that, all you have to do is to guard the safe house which has already been arranged for you and follow my instructions to the letter. I will handle your communications and direct negotiations for the ransom.'

'You want to use our group to carry out a filthy capitalist trick for an imperialist multinational?' Carlos sounded indignant.

'You must not look at it that way, Carlos. You and I know that. But if this is going to work, there is no reason why anyone else should know except a few people who are being bribed to keep silent about it. Your image must actually be quite the opposite. With my help, FART will have the status of the most important guerrilla movement in the Dominican Republic. The first to stage an international incident. You will receive press coverage, appear bigger than *Comandante Nueve* and the ELD.' Martin was now facing the entire group. 'And when the ransom is paid you will receive half a million dollars. We can guarantee police protection for all of you during the kidnapping, as long, of course, as you follow my instructions. What do you say? It's an opportunity that will not come again.'

Martin kept silent, listening to the reaction from around the table. *Cinco* and *Cuatro* seemed interested. *Tres* appeared noncommittal. *Dos* and Carlos were negative but in a surprised kind of way.

Carlos looked as if he were having second thoughts about having assembled the full committee to listen to Martin. 'It isn't right, *amigo*.'

Martin had Carlos on the spot and he was going to press the advantage. 'Is it right to live off teenage girls turning tricks in a whorehouse, Carlos? Is it right to scare people half to death who are doing nothing but quietly eating a hamburger at McDonald's? Look, Carlos, with the money and publicity you stand to gain by ripping off one of the biggest capitalist imperialist multinationals in the world, you can continue with your revolutionary activities at a much larger scale than before, becoming serious competition for the ELD or do whatever else you like. You all might decide that you want to go to Miami instead.' Martin could see that *Cinco* was really excited. 'Just remember what Lenin said: The capitalists will give us the rope with which to hang them. Carlos, I am offering you that rope.'

Martin had less than two weeks in which to plan the abduction and drill the FART into a believable kidnapping team. It had to look totally realistic while keeping the physical danger to the victim at a total minimum. Lopwitz would not inform them of who the intended target was until a few hours before his arrival in Santo Domingo.

It was decided to take the target as he was getting in or out of a rental car in his hotel parking lot, forcing him into a van which would pull up simultaneously. Martin modelled the operation on the abduction of the Texaco Vice President in Honduras over a month ago. Since FART and the Central American Workers Revolutionary Party, which carried out the Honduran kidnapping, shared similar names, this could even generate speculation that the groups were linked in some international conspiracy, a point in their favor during ransom negotiations.

Lopwitz would provide Martin with a prearranged schedule of John Clark's appointments in Santo Domingo for him to choose the best moment. It was decided beforehand, however, that the kidnapping should take place in broad daylight, the favored time of day for kidnappings. The size of FART was adequate for the abduction. Martin's research over the years indicated the average size of a terrorist assault team in most abductions to be around five persons.

The FART's arsenal appeared sufficient as well. The presence of a sub-machine-gun might add more weight to the incident. But if eyewitnesses saw pistols being waved at the victim, that would be standard enough, based on past precedents.

The presence of a woman among the kidnappers would also be useful. Martin's research indicated that the frequency of female involvement in terrorist kidnappings had more than doubled in the past five years. Women had played key roles in high-profile kidnappings in places as far apart as Colombia and West Germany. It was a female pushing a baby carriage that had facilitated the much publicized abduction of the Daimler Benz Corporate Chairman Hans Martin Schleyer in Frankfurt. It tricked the driver to bring Schleyer's limousine to a complete halt at an intersection, where the Red Army Faction awaited in ambush. *Cinco*, it was decided, would make the initial contact with the target, approaching him seductively to ask a favor, keeping him briefly distracted while the rest of the team went into action.

It was also decided that the van which would be used to pick up and transport the target should be painted up as a delivery vehicle. The van would also have to be abandoned at a certain point along their escape route and the victim transferred to a second vehicle for the final trek to the safe house. This was standard practice observed in most urban guerrilla kidnappings, and had to be followed for the operation to seem legitimate.

Martin rehearsed the voyage to the safe house with FART's *Tres*, the professional delivery driver. They went over it several times, making sure that he had the route memorized. The final stretch was over winding narrow roads into the hills. The driver had to try it four times before he managed the route without getting lost.

Meanwhile, Carlos and the other ex-medical student, *Dos*, experimented with the right dosage of barbiturates to keep the victim sedated for up to forty-eight hours without endangering his health. Lopwitz faxed over data on John Clark's medical history from the company's files in New York, with information on weight, blood type and so on.

Cuatro, the accountant, who was an amateur photographer, practiced taking pictures with a Polaroid camera. His role could become the most vital once the kidnapping was in progress.

After eleven days, they were prepared for a dress rehearsal. Martin played the victim. It went smoothly. Two days later, Lopwitz called Martin with the information he had been expecting: John Clark III, Vice President for international sales of the Sanitex Equipment Company, would be arriving in Santo Domingo within the next twenty-four hours. He would remain for a week, staying at the Hotel Lima in room 411. Sanitex Equipment had arranged a Hertz Renta-car. Martin also noted down Clark's appointments schedule.

John Clark III was finishing breakfast on his second day in Santo Domingo. With his second cup of strong black coffee, the haze in his eyes started clearing. But he still felt tired and miserable. Prior to his arrival here, he had spent three days in El Salvador and nearly a week in Guatemala. His stay in El Salvador had been cut short and he could only thank God for that. He'd been shocked that he'd actually been kept awake at night by the sound of gunfire, a routine occurrence, he had learned the next morning, as his car passed three dead bodies lying crumpled at a busy intersection: victims of death squads or left-wing guerrillas, nobody knew for sure.

He was relieved at the relative tranquility in Santo Domingo, although aware that the situation was deteriorating there as well. Jeeploads of helmeted, armed soldiers was the first sight that had struck him, the moment he'd gotten off the plane. The instructions from New York had been to proceed straight to Santo Domingo, leaving Eddie Hernandez, the Company's Latin American director, to handle Honduras on his own. They would join up again in Panama. It had been decided to split them up, to save traveling time, presumably. Clark did not know whether to be happy or depressed about a shortened trip. Despite the paranoid atmosphere of Central American revolutions coupled with the oppressive, humid heat and the depressing poverty of the region, he was still unsure if he could cope emotionally with what in all probability awaited him back home – divorcing Tiffany.

During his stay at the Metropolitan Club, Clark had tried to fight off his mounting depression with energetic games of squash and the company of friends. He had even tried dating another woman. But it had only ended up with a goodbye kiss on the cheek in the doorway to her apartment. He just could not bring himself to accept losing Tiffany and was unable to work up the strength to start up with someone else.

Clark checked his watch. It was time to leave for his appointment at the Ministry of Public Works. He made sure he had his car keys, picked up his briefcase and headed out through the lobby and into the humid heat. Although it was barely nine o'clock, the sun was already starting to beat down. He walked around the side of the hotel into the parking lot. As he reached his car he encountered a good-looking woman with a sizable chunk of thigh showing through the front slit of her dress. She wanted to know the time.

'*Las Nueve*,' Clark managed to say in Spanish.

She was all smiles. '*Americano, no?*'

A pick-up van pulled into the parking lot.

7

'**Y**es, I know, John. We are all just sick about it over here. But I'm sure we will get your son out safely. I took the precaution of insuring him through a Kidnapping and Ransom policy. A team of specialized negotiators should be on their way to the Dominican Republic . . . What? Yes, I've seen the papers . . . I know, he looks terrible.' Lopwitz glanced again at that morning's *New York Times* lying on his desk with the picture of a bedraggled John Clark III holding up a sign with the initials F.A.R.T. 'It doesn't mean the same thing in Spanish . . . at least we know he is alive.'

Lopwitz had known all kinds of fast workers before. But Martin took the prize. He should be recommended for an ambassadorship. Less than twenty-four hours after the taking of John Clark, UPI was distributing the photograph all over the world through its wire photo service together with a brief article quoting a terrorist statement that Martin had drafted:

. . . the previously little-known leftist urban guerrilla organization, Workers' Armed Revolutionary Front (FART), has claimed responsibility for the kidnapping. John Clark III was on a business trip representing his family-owned sanitation equipment company when he was 'taken prisoner' by the group.

In a lengthy manifesto delivered with the photograph, FART claims that the action is only the start of their 'offensive' against 'imperialist-supported oppression in the Dominican Republic'. The urban guerrilla group is demanding the lifting of martial law imposed after a recent anti-government demonstration in which over two dozen people were killed. FART blames the government for the deaths. Its other demands

81

include the release of all political prisoners and a ransom of forty million dollars.

The Dominican government claims to have little previous knowledge of FART. But police sources consider FART 'highly dangerous'. It has so far been credited with one major robbery and several other unresolved terrorist incidents in Santo Domingo. It is reported to have important international connections.

In its statement, FART claims 'solidarity' with all forces fighting 'imperialist conspiracies of capitalist multinationals and their lackeys'. Salvadoran guerrillas of the Frente Farabundo Marti de Liberacion in Central America, the PLO and Libya's Colonel Qadaffi are among those listed by the group as 'comrades in the common struggle'.

'No, John, I wouldn't necessarily put the blame on Howard, although I do agree that the trip was rather hastily planned . . . That's true, it was his idea. I remember raising some objections. Don't worry, as Corporate General Counsel, I will manage the crisis personally from this end. I'm putting together a team with . . . Well, he wasn't in a minute ago. But let me try again. Just a minute.'

Lopwitz buzzed Grover's secretary. 'Miss Preen, is Mr Grover in yet?'

'I'm sorry, Mr Lopwitz, but he hasn't arrived.'

'Please try again in about five minutes. If he is still not in, try his home.' It was strange that Grover should be so late, thought Lopwitz, especially in an emergency.

He spoke back into the phone. 'I'm sorry, John. But it seems that Howard is a bit late. Must have got stuck in traffic. I will have him call you the moment he gets in . . . Definitely, I agree that a general review of the company is in order once this is over . . . No, I don't think it's a good idea to send anyone else to Santo Domingo right now. It would be a useless risk. I will be in touch with the ransom negotiators by phone. If necessary, I will go down there myself . . . Thank you for your trust, John. I know this must be very hard on you and Kate. It's hard on all of us. Your son is such a fine young man . . . I can assure you that everything possible will be done to get him out . . . Yes, I will keep you posted on any new developments . . . Remember, it's best if you refrain from any direct public comment. Handle all your communications through me . . . Count on it, John, I will have Howard call you the moment he arrives . . . Well, don't be too hard on him, John. In a way we all share part of the blame. Very good, we will be in close touch.' Lopwitz put down the phone.

Things could not be going better. Grover would not survive this. As the ransom negotiations proceeded, Lopwitz would assume more direct control over the running of the company. He would be in a position to ease out Grover from the chairmanship and act unopposed when the moment came to approve a bail-out loan for the company that would effectively transfer majority ownership to a dummy offshore bank which he would be setting up with the twenty-million-dollar ransom. The tax-free money would have already been laundered through various accounts around the world. Lopwitz could sell off all the company's assets, and take the major share of the profits.

He emerged from his mental calculations to glance at his watch. The two insurance negotiators should have arrived in Santo Domingo by now. They should be calling him any moment. The light on his extension flashed. 'Mrs Grover on line three, Mr Lopwitz.'

'Put her on . . . Hello, Eileen, we were just . . . Oh! My God! . . .'

Howard Grover had just suffered a stroke.

8

About thirty feet under the ground of the Barriada del Pilar, one of the slums ringing Santo Domingo, *Comandante Nueve* paced nervously behind his metal desk in the recently completed underground bunker. It was connected to the outside through a series of interlocking tunnels. From here, the leader of the ELD was planning to direct the upcoming phase of an urban guerrilla insurrection against the government. His headquarters were equipped with printing presses, stores of arms, munitions and high explosives, a short-wave radio, his own battery-operated portable phone, closed-circuit television to guard all the approaches and a 'people's jail' to house some expected hostages.

Copies of several local and foreign newspapers were laid out across the *Comandante*'s desk. He was very upset at the headlines. A graduate of the Punto Cero military academy of Havana, who had distinguished himself fighting alongside the Sandinistas when the old dictatorship of Anastasio Somoza was overthrown in Nicaragua, *Comandante Nueve* could not accept that FART had now suddenly staged an important kidnapping.

'*Es inconcevible!*' *Nueve* slammed his fist against the dirt wall. His fury was such that it even gave a red tinge to his face which was otherwise the color of wet cement. He didn't get much sunshine. Whenever he had to move out of doors, he would do so by night.

His close confidante, Teresa, and his chief of information and coordination for Santo Domingo, *Comandante Cuatro*, sat before him in embarrassed silence. They were unable to offer any satisfactory explanation.

'Maybe it's a CIA trick,' said *Cuatro*, after a few tense seconds.

'Even the CIA could never have anything to do with a bunch of hopeless losers like FART.'

'I don't know what to say, *mi Comandante*.'

'I know what to say, you have not been doing your job. That's what to say. I told you to keep an eye on all leftist groups in Santo Domingo who might try to compete with us.'

'But after we rejected Carlos and his people because they disagreed with our tactics, none of us thought that they would add up to anything. We decided to ignore them. You yourself say that Carlos is about as revolutionary as Julio Iglesias.'

'Does not matter what I said, you had your task to perform and you have not done it.' The bearded revolutionary *Comandante* looked at *Cuatro* directly in the eyes, standing still now, beside his desk in camouflage fatigues and a red cravat. *Nueve* had a look that could strike primeval fear into people. Totally dedicated to the cause of revolutionary warfare, he did not drink, he did not smoke, he did not engage in promiscuous sex, although Teresa was known to be an occasional partner. He only lived and breathed the idea of imposing a Marxist–Leninist dictatorship in the Dominican Republic, following the example of Cuba. Nothing would deprive him of the dream of becoming the next Fidel Castro, although it was rumored that even the Cuban leader was somewhat afraid of him.

'We have worked for years to build up to the point we are reaching now, of striking a decisive blow against President Camuñas and his Yankee patrons. The men we sent to train in Nicaragua should be back any day. Cuba is promising to send us all the arms we need very soon. So we have been waiting and lying low. I have a list of over a dozen important people we have under surveillance who we could kidnap and hold prisoner right now. But we have not acted. Why? Because until we are really ready, it could bring on more pressure from the army than we could successfully cope with. So all this planning and discipline and caution and waiting – for what! So that the FART, that ridiculous group of Carlos and his gang of whores, can upstage me! So that those *Jiripollas* can appear in the international press as the main revolutionary movement in the Dominican Republic!'

'You should not worry so much,' said Teresa, 'the police will probably get them all soon and that will be the end of Carlos and FART.'

'Maybe,' said *Nueve*, 'and maybe not!' He slammed his fist again. 'The fact is that we don't know!' Was it possible that the Cubans were trying something behind his back? Maybe they wanted to unbalance him in some way. Those arms that Castro had been promising had not yet been sent. He had to get to the bottom of this.

He jabbed a finger at *Cuatro*. 'Your number-one priority is to get to the FART and find out where they are holding this John Clark.'

'As I'm sure you may be aware, gentlemen, my position concerning this matter is rather delicate.' Colonel Ventura toyed with his jade-handled letter opener as he faced the two dark-suited ransom negotiators, Brian Thorpe and Tom Cross, who had just arrived at the police headquarters from London. 'We are faced with a very serious terrorist threat in this country and FART is among the most dangerous urban guerrilla groups. I'm afraid to say that unless their demands are met, Mr Clark will in all probability be killed.'

'What's this group's track record exactly?' inquired Thorpe.

'My department has for some time been receiving information about a cell developing here linked to an international terrorist network. We have reason to believe that the leader of FART, this Carlos, received training in Libya. Until now, they had not been credited with any major incident, except for some preparatory attacks like the raid on the McDonald's restaurant. But it was believed that they were gearing up for a major strike. Now, we know what it was.'

'Why did they choose Mr Clark, do you suppose?'

'Well, in anticipation of a major kidnapping, we had increased security around all potential targets. Since Mr Clark had only just arrived for a short visit and we had not had the time to plan protection for him, we assume that they found him to be a convenient target of opportunity.'

'They must have a highly extensive intelligence network to know of his movements, and his arrival in only two days. His company can't be that well known,' said Cross, brushing back strands of his thinning blond hair.

'Yes, I am afraid so. FART is known to have informants placed everywhere. In the hotels, the public services, government ministries, most major foreign companies here, even in my own department. Mr Clark had made an appointment to see our Minister of Public Works on the morning in which he was kidnapped, well in advance of his arrival. It was known where he was going to be staying. It is to be assumed that a mole in the Ministry provided the information to FART. We are seriously investigating that possibility.'

'Are there any eyewitnesses to the actual abduction?' It was Thorpe again.

'Yes. The doorman of the hotel and another of the guests say they saw Mr Clark being forced into a laundry van by a woman and two or three men dressed in overalls. They were carrying pistols. One had a rifle. The van was abandoned about a mile away, where they changed to another vehicle. Inside the van we found a used syringe. Mr Clark was most probably drugged with a tranquilizer. It's all in the police reports that I gave you. Would you care to inspect the evidence?'

'Later, certainly. Now our priority is to decide exactly how we are going to handle this.' Thorpe and Cross looked at each other. This was going to be a difficult one. They had worked together on many kidnapping cases before, all over the world. But this was their first time in the Dominican Republic. Both of them had served in the British army, Cross as an intelligence officer assigned to M.I.5 and Thorpe as a paratrooper with the Special Air Service, where he reached the rank of Captain. If the nature of their current work was less physically stressing when compared to military service in such places as Aden and Ulster, the extreme psychological pressures under which they had to labor more than compensated. They could never be totally certain of anything they did, always trying to calculate imponderables; rarely able to be sure of how much a terrorist demand was bluff and how much real. Always balancing the various conflicting interests that converged in a kidnapping: those of the company or family of the victim who would want him back alive at any cost, those of the underwriters for the insurance whose priority would be to pay up as little as possible, those of the terrorists who had to be satisfied either way. And last but not least, those of the local authorities whose political imperatives would invariably come into play.

Upon checking into the Hotel Lima, Thorpe had immediately notified Lopwitz of their arrival. The somber-sounding Corporate Chief Counsel told them that he had already communicated with the kidnappers who were publicly demanding a ransom of forty million dollars as well as political concessions from the Dominican government. Lopwitz was of the opinion that FART would lower its ransom demand if serious negotiations were entered into immediately. And so it would have to be, thought Thorpe. There was nothing they could do about the political concessions, Clark's insurance only covered him for twenty-four and a half million and any final settlement should be considerably below that.

'You will, of course, realize that there is nothing our government can do to meet the terrorist demands,' said Ventura, reclining in the leather chair. 'Quite the contrary, our *Presidente* was considering lifting martial law before the kidnapping. Now it is out of the question. We have to be absolutely firm with terrorists. There is not the slightest chance of meeting any of the political demands or even negotiating token concessions.' He stood and moved towards the window. 'I realize that your job is to ransom Mr Clark. To be very frank with you, neither I nor anyone else in the government wish to have a dead American businessman on our hands.'

'Does that mean that you are prepared to cooperate with us?'

'I am giving you as much direct cooperation as I can give you, Mr Thorpe. My men are, naturally, doing all that can be done to find where FART is keeping Mr Clark.' He looked out at groups of his men mingling in the dusty courtyard of his drab fortress. 'I have ordered them to concentrate in certain slum districts around the city where we have reason to believe the terrorist safe house may be located.' Ventura turned back from the window to face the two Englishmen. 'I am prepared to allow you to work unhindered for now. But I suggest that you proceed quickly and quietly. If this affair drags on, there are elements in our army which may at any moment apply pressure on me and the government to stop any private negotiations for a ransom.'

Frank Burns, the Regional Security Officer at the US Embassy, sat on top of his desk with his legs hanging almost to the floor. A former FBI man, he was now the State Department official responsible for the physical safety of US Embassy personnel and other American citizens in the Dominican Republic. With him were the CIA Station Chief, Michael Webb, and the Deputy Station Chief, Steven Drysdale.

'We should have stayed on top of this group FART,' Burns was saying. 'But who the hell would have guessed that a bunch of guys with a name like that, who have done nothing so far except freeload on Big Macs, would stage the first major kidnapping of a US citizen in Santo Domingo.'

'It's a goddam smelly FART if you ask me.' Webb started to laugh but quickly realized that humor was not quite in order. He cleared his throat. 'I realize that it does not mean the same thing in Spanish.'

The RSO crossed his ankles. 'It was not even among the groups that I listed in my last report to Washington. It's goddam embarrassing.'

'This has happened lots of times before, Frank,' Webb said, trying to sound comforting.

'I realize, Mike, but when it does happen the guys back at the Office for Combating Terrorism don't like it. This new guy Crayton they've named to head it is hell-bent on upgrading our reporting system. Counter-terrorist intelligence has now taken priority. Crayton was on the phone from Washington this morning chewing my ass out.'

'What do the local cops say?' asked Drysdale.

'When I spoke to them after the McDonald's incident over a month ago, they didn't ascribe any importance to FART. Now they are saying that it's a very dangerous group trained in Libya and all that shit. When I called Colonel Ventura he said that they had received additional intelligence about the group only a week ago, after he and I had our weekly meeting. He apologized, can you believe it, he apologized for not having informed us in advance.'

'Where the hell did he get his intelligence?' This was Webb. 'Until now he has been getting most of it from us. We were the ones who told him about the ELD guys going to train in Nicaragua – over your objections, Drysdale.'

'Well, it hardly seems that we got back our favor, Mike. We risk compromising our sources and the police just turn around and let us get caught with our pants down in the first big hit on an American.' Drysdale was of a new breed of CIA officer who strongly believed in developing agents inside Third World revolutionary movements and protecting them even at the expense of the interests of dubious allies.

'They are just inefficient, Drysdale, don't try reading any more into it.' Webb loosened his necktie and unbuttoned his collar.

'That's always been my point, why should we constantly throw in our lot with corrupt, inefficient losers?'

'If we trained and equipped them better, maybe they would not be so goddam inefficient.'

'Don't you get tired of repeating the same old refrain, Mike?'

'Listen, Drysdale, if your friends on the far left are so goddam helpful, how come you don't have anything on this FART group?'

Webb had struck a raw nerve in Drysdale. He had been sent to the Dominican Republic for a chance to test out his theories about building American support inside Third World revolutionary movements but had little to show after six months of effort. He had just one mid-level source in ELD and effective control over only one small university-based leftist group which would have little or no influence if it ever came to a full-scale revolutionary upheaval. Drysdale could only fall back on the usual clichés. 'If we were not so bent on upholding the status quo those who are for some real change in their societies might be more disposed to . . .'

Burns took the opportunity to cut off the argument. 'Bill, please. I didn't bring you in here for a policy debate. Now look, I've got two British guys who have been sent down by Lloyds to negotiate a ransom for Clark coming around to see me in about an hour and then I have to brief the Ambassador. What am I supposed to tell them?'

'Just go along with what the police say.' Webb lit a cigarette.

'You mean that FART is Libyan-trained and all that?'

'Unless we have evidence to the contrary, I see no reason to contradict them.' He took a deep drag.

'What is our position on private negotiations to ransom an American?'

'Hell, Frank, you should have the answer to that, not me.' Webb exhaled. 'The CIA is not a law enforcement agency.'

Roger MacPhearson, Executive Producer of the NBN's *Evening News*, presided over his daily production meeting dressed in blue jeans and cowboy boots. 'I hope you all realize that CBS just kicked the shit out of us in Central America. They had a camera team in place in the south of El Salvador when FMLN guerrillas attacked that army base. They got some of the best combat footage since Vietnam. All we have is some fucking farm cooperative burning down somewhere east of the capital, without even a dead body. The peasants had fled the place before the guerrillas arrived. All that the FMLN found when they entered the farm was Burton Simms, his cameraman and the soundman.' MacPhearson's voice strained just slightly. 'Burt tells me that he actually had to bribe the guerrillas to shoot off some rounds from their AK-47s so that our viewers wouldn't confuse the scene with some brush fire in Arkansas. How do you explain this, Jeff?' MacPhearson threw a look at the News Director.

'Well, Roger, our stringer in San Salvador told Simms and his team that the main rebel offensive was going to come in the east. He had some advance knowledge that the farm cooperative was going to be a target. The problem is that the Salvadoran army didn't bother to defend it.'

'Look, guys.' MacPhearson glanced around the table. 'We just have to get our act together in Central America.' He slung one of his booted legs over the side of his chair. 'It's potentially the hottest story since Vietnam and our coverage so far has been, quite frankly, shitty.'

The news anchorman, Chet Hinkley, agreed. 'The last time there was some heavy shooting down there on the border between Nicaragua and Honduras, ABC got the story. We had to content ourselves with a C-130 landing paratroops in Tegucigalpa.'

'I've decided to send a second team with Jane Winter to El Salvador.' MacPhearson placed his feet squarely on top of the conference table, reclining in his chair. He sipped coffee from a large mug.

'It could already be too late, Roger.' It was the anchorman. 'Since the Pentagon rushed down those Cobra helicopter gunships to the Salvadoran army, the rebel offensive has died down.'

'So what do you suggest we do?'

'There's trouble in a lot of countries down there. What we should do is try to pre-empt the other networks when the next crisis breaks out.'

'Do you carry a crystal ball, Chet?'

'Not a crystal ball, Roger. But we know the shit is hitting the fan in the Dominican Republic, for example.'

'That's where we landed the Marines twenty years ago, isn't it?'

'That's right, and we seem to be getting some fun and games there again. Martial law was declared a month ago after anti-government demonstrators were massacred by government troops and an American businessman has just been kidnapped in Santo Domingo by a terrorist group called FART.'

'FART?' MacPhearson let out a deep belly laugh. 'That's a story in itself.'

'So why don't we re-route Jane Winter and her camera team to Santo Domingo?'

MacPhearson rubbed his chin. 'That's a thought.'

9

B rian Thorpe and Tom Cross got back to the Hotel Lima after a pleasant lunch at an Italian restaurant recommended to them by Frank Burns. In his room Thorpe found a large envelope which had been slipped under his door. He opened it up and called Cross. It was the first direct communication from the kidnappers with a photograph of Clark holding up a copy of that day's newspaper and a note written in block letters on a sheet of paper with FART's logo of a six-pointed star superimposed on the initials. According to the note, the group was willing to take up its political demands with the government at a later stage. They would release Clark if a ransom of forty million dollars was paid in seventy-two hours.

'At least they are prepared to be reasonable.' Both he and Thorpe had shed their coats and ties. 'I'm sure they will settle for half of what they are asking. Twenty million would fall in neatly within Clark's insurance coverage.'

'I think that's too much,' Thorpe objected. 'At this stage anyway.'

'Do you think that there is any question about the validity of the kidnapping?'

'I think Clark's definitely been kidnapped all right.' Thorpe fished out two bottles of mineral water from the mini-refrigerator and handed one to Cross. 'I'm just not convinced about the strength of this group FART. For all we know they could be holding on by their fingertips and would eagerly accept a far lower ransom than twenty million. Don't forget that our primary responsibility is to the insurance company, Tom.'

'But both the police and the American Embassy maintain that the group is very dangerous, trained in Libya and so on.'

'How can we possibly confirm that, Tom? I can't imagine that the intelligence capabilities of the police here are exactly the most reliable.' Thorpe seated himself by the balcony window, taking a long swig from the bottle. 'The Americans are obviously just going along with what the police have told them. Burns admitted that they did not know much about the group before yesterday.'

'You think that there is more than meets the eye?'

'Or less. The fact is that our information people in London did not have a record on any terrorist group in the Dominican Republic except this Dominican Liberation army, ELD. The briefing they gave us quoted a report put out a month ago by Security International which anticipated the kidnapping of a foreign executive here. But it said nothing about any FART.'

'I honestly think that if these people are ready to bargain, we should get our man out as soon as possible. Let's take advantage of the fact that Ventura is allowing us a free hand. He did say that interference could arise from the part of the military. I don't want to end up in jail the way we did in Colombia. Let's not have that again.'

'We will just have to take our chances, Tom. Before we make any offer to the FART, I just think that we should do some investigating ourselves. This group simply does not strike me as being powerful enough to command one of the highest ransoms ever paid in Central America.'

'All the hallmarks of the kidnapping point to a highly professional job as far as I can see, and the group is obviously not afraid of exposure.'

'True. But judging from FART's performance until now, it seems to go exclusively after soft unprotected targets. Robbing a McDonald's isn't exactly storming Fort Knox.'

'That fits the pattern of most terrorist groups, Brian, they very rarely storm Fort Knox. Remember that Libyan-backed Palestinian network which did nothing except throw hand-grenades into crowded cafés until it joined up with the Red Army Faction and took all of the OPEC oil ministers hostage in Vienna.'

'I realize what you are saying, Tom. But we have to find out more about this FART ourselves. If it's as serious a threat as they say it is, or connected with ELD, we can offer something close to Clark's full coverage. If it's not, any ransom must be considerably lower.'

Martin lay on his bed two floors above, wishing that he could overhear the conversation which the two ransom negotiators would be having once they found the message he had slipped under Thorpe's door. His communication arrangement with FART was moving along smoothly enough. It had been decided that all five members would remain at the villa with Clark for the duration of the kidnapping. Clark needed to be guarded as closely as possible. If he tried to escape they would have to subdue him bodily; firing anything other than a warning shot was out of the question. It was equally necessary to avoid any breach of security caused by members of the group remaining too long on the outside. Not that it had taken much persuasion to convince Carlos and his people to enjoy a few weeks in a beautiful country villa with colour television, swimming pool, all the luxuries and plenty of space for target practice. Martin, who had now rented a car, planned to drop by occasionally to check things out, remaining in constant contact by phone.

Only one of the FART, *Cuatro* or Luis, would be

coming into Santo Domingo with any regularity. He needed to continue putting in some hours at his regular job, and as photographer he might need to buy film or other equipment for his camera. He would be in charge of all the shopping as well. The safe house had to remain well stocked with food and drink for Clark's comfort as well as everyone else's.

Luis would also relay to Martin the photographs of Clark to pass on to the press and the ransom negotiators. They would be left in double-sealed envelopes at Casa Las Familias where Graciela would pick them up and bring them to Martin's hotel room. When they needed to be released to the press, Graciela would drop them at a pre-arranged spot – a certain garbage can had already been selected – near the office of UPI. Martin would tell the UPI man where he could pick them up, by an anonymous phone call.

The negotiators, for their part, would be instructed in Martin's messages to leave written replies in a sealed envelope wrapped in plastic inside the cistern of the left-hand toilet booth of the men's room in the hotel lobby. An adequate place for a FART, if ever there was one, Martin had thought to himself.

Graciela had naturally been scared at first by her assignment, especially after Martin told her what it involved. But he had assured her that nothing could happen to her and she confessed that she was prepared to do anything he wanted. Martin was now expecting the measured four knocks on the door with some anticipation. She had needed to rush out that morning to pick up the photographs at Casa Las Familias and there had not been enough time to give him his morning treat. After bringing them to his room before lunch, she had to rush out again to put in her usual two hours at one of her father's shops. A certain swelling inside his pants needed her attention.

The phone rang. Martin picked it up. It was Lopwitz. 'Yes, Herb ... When, tonight? ... In the bar downstairs, eight o'clock . . . Yes, I think I can find my way out to the house at night . . . She will be wearing a green dress and ask me to buy her a strawberry daquiri . . . Herb, can you give me an idea what this is about? . . . Oh, I see . . . No, no news yet. I delivered the message to them only an hour ago . . . Yes, definitely. I'll meet your friend tonight.'

The next morning, Tom Cross was in the office of the commander of police intelligence, Major Otero, inquiring further into FART

'So you are telling me that before they robbed McDonald's you had nothing on this group?'

'It was the first time it came to our attention but we managed to link it to other acts of terrorism in Santo Domingo and started to investigate it.'

'How did you find out that certain members of the group were trained in Libya?'

'That information came from the top.'

'Did you have any intelligence to the effect that they were preparing to stage a kidnapping?'

'Not a kidnapping exactly, perhaps, but we could deduce that they were preparing for a major attack. It was a relatively new group, and we had no time to develop much inside knowledge on its activities or plans.'

'Do you think that FART is connected with ELD?'

'As far as we know there is no connection.' Otero was starting to get annoyed. 'I cannot tell you any more than what I have said already. Terrorist movements are gaining strength here in the Dominican Republic; new groups are developing all the time. We are investigating the kidnapping. But until we make further headway, I have nothing more to say.'

Brian Thorpe was not having much more luck with a well-known radical priest he had gone to see. Padre Mejia ran a 'human rights' monitoring organization reputed to have extensive contacts with the underground left. In other kidnapping cases Thorpe had handled in Latin America, men like Padre Mejia often served as intermediaries for guerrilla networks.

'My organization has had absolutely no contact with FART, nor do I personally know anything about the group. I can assure you that I would be more than glad to be of help. But I do not have any information which could be of use. I can only remember very vaguely one of my brothers telling me about a young man he had spoken to once, called Carlos, I think, who had been involved with ELD and was forming a separate revolutionary group with a name having something to do with Workers' Armed Front. I do not remember exactly to be perfectly honest.'

'Do you remember who told you?'

'I am afraid I don't.'

'Are there other organizations such as yours here in Santo Domingo which might be able to provide me with more information?'

'Yes, you can try others.' He called through the open door of his office to one of his assistants. 'Teresa!'

Brian Thorpe now got a front view of the attractive, dark-haired woman in tight black T-shirt and short skirt whom he had noticed bending over the filing cabinet when he entered the office some twenty minutes earlier. She seemed very light-skinned for a Dominican.

'This is Mr Brian Thorpe,' Padre Mejia said.

She shook his hand. 'How do you do?'

'Mr Thorpe has been sent here from London to negotiate a ransom to rescue the life of the American who was kidnapped the day before yesterday. He needs information about the group FART. Please provide him with the particulars of other Catholic organizations such as ours which may be of help to him.'

The priest and Thorpe stood up simultaneously. 'I'm sorry that I cannot be of any further assistance to you, Mr Thorpe. But I am sure Teresa will help you. I hope that you succeed in your mission.'

When Thorpe sat down across Teresa's desk, she wrote down an address on a slip of paper and smiled at him. 'Meet me here tonight at eight-thirty. We can have dinner. I will tell you all there is to know about FART.'

Nora pulled in a cart with a tray of food, walked up to the bed and helped him to sit up. 'Where am I? What's happened?' He could barely get the words out.

'It will be explained later. For the moment just eat your food. You must be hungry.'

Clark willingly agreed. He picked up the bowl of chicken broth and drank it down. She buttered some bread for him as he attacked his second course of a juicy slice of tenderloin steak with boiled vegetables and rice. He had difficulty cutting the meat. His hands kept trembling. Nora helped him. As he satisfied his hunger, the numbness receded, the warmth of nourishment filling his cold stomach. 'What did you say your name was?' He still could not get his voice above a loud whisper.

'Nora.' She continued to smile, a reassuring smile. 'Now finish your food, you are not well.'

'Where am I?'

She caressed his hair with her long fingers. 'I assure you that you are going to be all right.' She kissed him gently on the mouth, a warm tingling wet kiss.

Could he have died and gone to heaven? Clark thought to himself briefly. He now noticed her beautiful cleavage.

When he had finished his food, she passed him a glass of water and a pill. 'Take this. It will make you feel better.'

He did as he was told.

'You must rest some more for now, turn around.'

He turned face down on his pillow, and she started massaging his back, the neck, around the shoulders. It felt fantastic. A different kind of numbness now crept into him. Not the numbness of being unable to feel but, rather, the numbness which came with avoiding any thought which might disturb the pleasure which now came over him.

Soon, Clark had drifted back to sleep. The pill would put him out for another six hours.

Teresa looked out into the gathering purple dusk. Placid Caribbean wavelets swept up gently on to the powdered white beach that stretched out for several meters in front. The beach club restaurant of the resort hotel of La Romana was surrounded on the other three sides by a thick tropical garden. She sipped a glass of white wine, enjoying the scents on the warm breeze.

When she was only eight, Teresa had been abandoned by her American father, an adventurous mining entrepreneur in Chile who had run out of luck. She was brought up in Santiago by her mother, who never remarried and made a modest living teaching English. Teresa never fully recovered psychologically from her early sense of loss. During the Allende years she had joined the extreme leftist Movimiento de Izquierda Revolucionaria (MIR). When just turned seventeen, she became the mistress of one of MIR's main leaders, Andres Sandoval, who was charged with the task of arming a 'popular army' in the slums of Santiago with weapons sent from Cuba. When General

Pinochet launched his violent coup, Sandoval was among the first to be arrested and shot.

Teresa managed to flee, traveling to Europe and joining up with radical leftist exiles from all over Latin America. In Paris, London, Rome and elsewhere she was helped financially and in other ways by the Junta de Coordinacion Revolucionaria, an international network formed with money the Argentine People's Revolutionary Army (ERP) had raised through ransoming business executives. She toured Europe in considerable luxury.

When the Sandinistas toppled Somoza in 1978 Teresa went to Central America. Her fluent English proved useful at the Sandinistas' press office which had the vital task of swaying public sympathy in the United States and Europe behind their cause. In Nicaragua, she met Arturo Cayentano and followed him to the Dominican Republic where he became leader and *Comandante Nueve* of the Ejercito de Liberacion Dominicano (ELD). Her function as an above-ground propagandist and agent of influence was important to the ELD. When she informed *Comandante Nueve* of her chance encounter at Padre Mejia's office that morning, he was all in favor of her getting to know Brian Thorpe and finding out all she could about any ransom negotiations with FART.

Thorpe arrived at the table a few minutes late, explaining that he had gotten somewhat lost on his drive from the center of Santo Domingo. They exchanged a few pleasantries over chilled white wine as Thorpe remarked on the beauty of the restaurant's location. He refrained from asking what a Chilean was doing working for leftist causes in the Dominican Republic. He could half guess. He had met a few like Teresa before.

'So you are here to offer a ransom for John Clark?'

Thorpe nodded. The menus arrived. She quickly put hers aside, ordering a seafood salad. He ordered some fresh oysters for both of them and grilled sword-fish for his second course.

'How much are you offering?' There was a very intense quality about her.

'I'm afraid I can't tell you that. Suffice it to say that Mr Clark is covered by insurance. I am under contract with the underwriters to negotiate a payment for his release.' He sipped his wine without taking his eyes off her. She was wearing a low-cut knitted dress. Thick brown hair framed her finely chiselled face, which did not carry a trace of make-up. 'You tell me that you have some information on this group FART.'

'I can tell you more about it than anyone else whom you are likely to talk to.'

'Please do.'

'First I want to know how much ransom you are offering for Clark.'

If Teresa was in some remote way connected with FART or talked to the newspapers, anything he said could prejudice the negotiations. 'I'll be perfectly frank with you, Teresa. I have not myself decided how much to offer. You have, surely, read the papers. They are asking forty million dollars. The insurance cover-age is considerably below that. How much we actually offer depends on a variety of factors such as the capa-bilities of FART.'

Teresa figured it would be in the interests of the ELD to tell Thorpe what they knew. 'It's a very small group. We think they don't exceed more than half a dozen people.'

'Who is we?'

'I am connected with the largest underground revolutionary network in this country.'

'You mean the ELD?'

Teresa nodded.

'I was being led to believe that FART was a highly dangerous group. That its leader, this Carlos, was trained in Libya. I was also getting the impression that

FART could be a faction or a front for the ELD.'

'The FART has nothing to do with the ELD.'

The oysters arrived. Thorpe and Teresa took one each, using their teeth to scoop out the meat from the shells.

'Then who are they?'

'Carlos and a few of his friends tried to join the ELD more than a year ago. He was then a medical student. They were rejected, not found to be disciplined enough.'

'So then one is to assume that he established some different connection, went to train in Libya and returned to form his own group.'

'We doubt it. The leader of ELD, *Comandante Nueve*, does not understand how it is possible that Carlos and FART could have pulled off this kidnapping.'

'The fact is that they have and so far it looks like a highly professional job. They must have got backing from somewhere.'

'We are sure that none of them has ever left the Dominican Republic.'

'How can you be sure?'

'We just know. Carlos is not a serious Marxist revolutionary. He is involved in prostitution. He is just a common delinquent.'

'Have you people been keeping track of FART? From what you tell me, this kidnapping came as something of a surprise.'

'We know their background. Right now, we are making every effort to find out more.'

Thorpe sipped his wine and was silent for a few minutes. 'I'll tell you what, Teresa. You keep me informed on anything you find out about FART and we may be able to exchange some information.' He stretched his hand to deal a handshake. She squeezed his palm, entwining her fingers with his.

John Clark awoke suddenly. As he turned in his bed, the door opened and she appeared, just as he remembered her. She gently closed the door and approached him, her perfect curves silhouetted in the half-light.

She sat beside him on the bed and crossed her shiny thighs. 'Remember me? I'm Nora.' Clark remained speechless. 'You want me?' she inquired. 'You can have me. If you do exactly as I say. You can have all of me, if you just accept and ask no questions.' In his desire, Clark could think of no questions. She licked her lips, tossed her long thick dark hair and eased off the thin straps of her gown.

Brian Thorpe was on his second cup of coffee that morning, having a working breakfast in his room with Tom Cross. 'Don't misunderstand me, Tom, the fact that according to Teresa the ELD is disowning FART by no means renders them harmless. Quite the contrary, without a large organization sustaining them, Clark's captors might even act more unpredictably.'

'What do you suggest then?'

'Let's offer them ten million dollars. I've thought about it. The idea of intriguing around a little longer to secure a lower ransom has occurred to me. But I agree with you that we should go for a quick settlement.'

Thorpe had spent the night at La Romana with Teresa, the warmth of her sex some hours earlier encouraging his desire for yet more of the 'mutual exchange' he had proposed over dinner. But the headlines in that morning's papers which lay before him had a sobering effect. Two police patrols had been ambushed the previous evening, in Santo Domingo's slums, while in the process of searching for John Clark. Some six policemen had been killed and another two badly wounded. The burned carcasses of a jeep and a radio car were displayed in large black and white photographs on the front page.

Any delay in getting John Clark out alive would be inexcusable. Even if ten million might seem excessive for a group as obscure as FART, such amounts were being paid out to ransom kidnapped businessmen elsewhere in Central America, held by groups not much better known than FART. If those holding Clark had studied such recent cases, there was little reason to suppose that they would settle for much less.

Whatever reasons Teresa or the ELD might have for downplaying FART – which was, in essence, an ELD splinter faction – they could not be allowed to influence his own judgment. Teresa had confirmed the one factor which ultimately mattered most: FART, as a terrorist group, existed.

'Get out some stationery, Tom, and type out a note to say that we will offer ten million dollars as soon as we have proof that Clark is still alive. They may suggest methods of payment. Deliver it to the drop as soon as possible.'

'Should one of us try to observe who picks it up?'

'Unless you wish to hang around the men's lavatory all day, I wouldn't bother.'

'Any calls, Jill?' It was after lunch and Herbert Lopwitz was slipping out of his camelhair overcoat as he entered the Chairman's office, which he had now moved into. He had just returned from seeing Howard Grover at the hospital. The medical prognosis following bypass surgery was that Grover would live. But he needed complete rest for several months. Lopwitz was now the company's acting Chairman.

The secretary handed Lopwitz several pink message

slips. As he proceeded into the spacious inner office, the view of Park Avenue which opened in front of him showed Grand Central Station's turn-of-the-century façade at the base of the Pan Am building.

He looked through the messages, hoping to see one from Santo Domingo. The last call he had from Martin was after he had dropped off Nora at the safe house. There were less than twenty-four hours to go before the three-day deadline expired. Martin had done such a perfect job, it was just possible that he might get everything that he had bargained for, Lopwitz thought.

As he picked up the phone to return a call from an important client in California, the light flashed on one of the other extensions. He pressed the button down. 'Long-distance for you, Mr Lopwitz, from Santo Domingo.'

'I'll take it.'

It was Martin's voice.

'Let me call you back in twenty minutes.' He hung up the phone and spoke into the intercom. 'I have to go out urgently, Jill. Please have my limousine waiting at the front entrance.'

Lopwitz ascended the red carpeted elevator to the eleventh floor of his Fifth Avenue apartment building. The door slid open on to the checker-tiled landing. He turned the key to his front door and entered his tastefully decorated apartment with its oriental rugs and antiques. He had lived mostly alone here since his divorce three years ago. His daughter sometimes visited, as did other types of female company. Diagonally across the wide vestibule was a small den-study. He sat behind the desk which gave on to a view of Central Park, picked up the phone and dialed direct to the Hotel Lima in Santo Domingo.

'Room 411, please.' It rang once and Martin picked it up.

'. . . Ten million?' Lopwitz's heart sank. 'That's not nearly enough, Martin. I told you that I have to clear twenty and gross one or two above that . . . I agree that it's a good sign that they have replied with an offer a day before the deadline expires. It shows that they are convinced; that's essential. You've done a good job. But we will have to bargain a bit harder. Let me call Colonel Ventura. I'll get right back to you.'

After speaking with Lopwitz again that afternoon, Martin got into his car and drove out to the villa where they were holding Clark. Past the airport, he kept going on a mostly even line, passing white sandy beaches on one side and large expanses of tobacco and sugar-cane fields on the other. Silhouetted behind the growing fields were the hills and mountains that took up much of the island's interior.

After driving through the wealthy resort area of La Romana, with its walled-in villas and polo fields, he cut right into a narrower interior road, straight through agricultural land, heavily scented with the smell of fresh fertilizer. The road eventually began winding around the foothills of the Sierra, over valleys rich with tropical vegetation. At a dirt-crossing marked by bunched palm trees, he cut a right again. The bumpy, unpaved road, still muddy in parts from recent rainfalls, went on for almost two miles. In the thickening forest a sign read Plantacion de Arguelles. There, he turned for the final stretch. After going two hundred yards, he drove into a man-made clearing. On an elevation stood the Spanish-style 'Cortijo' with its red-tiled roofs greening with moss and yellowing white walls in need of paint. The natural beauty of the spot was accentuated by the pink-purple glow of a Caribbean sunset.

Martin was pleased to see FART's *Tres* sitting guard on the outside porch, reclined on a chair while holding the group's heavy artillery, the sawn-off double-barrel shotgun. He wondered if Carlos had put on the show to impress him. *Tres* mocked a military salute as Martin went past.

Carlos awaited him in the living-room like a grand *señor* with a bottle of rum, Coca-Cola and an ice bucket on the table. The large inner space opened up into grounds, at the back of which he noticed *Cinco* bathing topless in the swimming pool.

Martin fixed himself a 'Cuba libre' and sat on the large armchair opposite Carlos, proceeding to inform him about the good news and the bad news. A new counter-offer would be made to the insurance people, reducing the demand to thirty million. But it would have to be accompanied by some dramatic act to convince the negotiators to settle for no less than twenty.

Carlos toyed pensively with his beard. 'What do you suggest we do?'

'We have to do something that is at once dramatic, does not expose any of us and won't cause direct bloodshed. I would say that narrows the possibilities down to a bombing. Can you work with explosives, Carlos?'

'I know how we can make a good bomb using dynamite and a tank of butane gas. We strap the dynamite to the gas tank and the force of the explosion ruptures it, releasing the pressurized flammable gas and vaboom! Like the *bomba atomica*.'

'Good thinking. Now the question is where are we going to plant it. I was thinking of the Hotel Lima. But that would bring too much pressure on me there. Besides, somebody could get killed.'

'It could be a car bomb outside the hotel.'

'Could be. But wouldn't it be more convincing for a terrorist group to choose a target for its political significance instead of just trying to impress a couple of ransom negotiators? Besides, these two guys are former British army, they are probably familiar with explosives. If they actually see the explosion or closely inspect the damage, they may conclude that it's only dynamite and butane. We want them to think that it's some powerful plastic like Semtex which you would have acquired from Libya.'

'I have an idea.' Carlos rose up. 'The Plaza de la Catedral is always deserted at night. Just on the corner of the avenida are the offices of Chase Manhattan Bank. That's our target. We'll say that it's a warning to all capitalist multinationals and threaten to kill Clark.'

Just as Martin was about to congratulate Carlos on his excellent plan, Nora came down the stairway stark-naked. She blew a kiss at Martin and disappeared into the kitchen. Martin had had a taste of her the other night on their drive from Santo Domingo. Clark should be a very happy hostage. 'How are they getting along, by the way?'

'They've been screwing solidly since yesterday. You should see the pictures.'

There was a two-way mirror into Clark's bedroom.

Juan Porras lay naked on the brass bed in one of the back rooms of Casa Las Familias. He smoked a cigarette as Pepita pulled her flimsy dress back on. They had just finished a brief session.

'So, you say that you know Carlos.'

'Yes.' The girl adjusted her bosom.

'Do you know where he is? I am an old friend. I need to find him.' Porras was actually the District Coordinator for the ELD. His duties included collection of 'revolutionary taxes' – protection money – from local businesses, and information gathering.

'I have not seen him for a while. I don't know where he is.' She moved indifferently towards the night table to pick up the money he had put down for her. As her hand reached for the hundred-peso bill, Porras grabbed her arm, slung her down on the bed and slapped her hard on the face. 'Tell me where he is, you *puta*, or I will tell your father what you do here and have him give you a much worse beating.'

'I told you the truth! I don't know. I have not seen him for more than a week. Nobody has.' She was trying to hold back the tears.

'Have you seen any of his friends, any other members of his group FART?' He shook her. 'Answer me.' He raised his palm again.

She covered her face, screaming 'Yes!' between sobs. 'One of his group, Luis, he has been in a couple of times. He leaves –' more sobs '– he has been leaving messages with the barman.'

The long-haired blonde with the star quality stepped out of the Mercedes as it pulled up in front of the hotel. Two men, emerging from the same car, followed her in loaded down with heavy equipment. Several bellboys took care of the rest of the luggage.

The concierge promptly attended her at the reception desk.

'I'm Jane Winter of *NBN Evening News* in Washington. I believe that some rooms have been reserved for me and my crew.' The throaty femininity of her voice was the trademark of US television's fastest-rising news correspondent. She was the favorite of Executive Producer Roger MacPhearson, who had originally discovered her as a local newscaster in Dallas.

'Yes, of course, *señora*. How long do you expect to stay?'

In the Piano Lounge, Steven Drysdale was into his second Scotch on the rocks. Despite his best efforts, including generous pay-offs to a group at the university, there was 'no trace of a FART', as he ironically put it to himself.

Drysdale had come to Santo Domingo with high hopes. 'If only we can ride Third World revolutions instead of always getting caught under the breaking wave there will be no more Vietnams,' he had preached up and down the corridors at Langley. His zealous views earned him as many enemies as friends among the Agency's big thinkers. It had been decided to give him a chance, and six months ago he had arrived in Santo Domingo with the exalted status for his age – he was just thirty-six – of Deputy Chief of Station. But now that the revolution was about to break, Drysdale had little to show for all his bluster.

If anyone was caught under a wave, it was him. He had just come from a clandestine meeting with the only agent which the CIA had developed inside the ELD, a district coordinator who had been compromised through his fondness for little boys. But there was little to add, only that *Comandante Nueve* was reported to be quite upset about the kidnapping. This source was convinced that FART was in no way coordinating its activities with ELD. That blew the theory that Drysdale had tried to impress upon his Station Chief, Mike Webb, that FART was a front group.

If this went on much longer, Drysdale's days in Santo Domingo were numbered. And if the Dominican Republic turned into another Cuba or a Nicaragua, he could probably look forward to a dusty desk job back in Langley amongst the archives. He drained his second Scotch and glanced at his watch. The person he was expecting should be arriving soon.

A few stools down from where Drysdale sat, Martin was nervously drinking a rum and Coke. He could spot the two ransom negotiators sitting in quiet conversation at one of the corner tables. He thought of sitting near them to try and pick up on what they might be saying. But that would be too risky. Perhaps if he got one of the ladies-in-waiting to sit with him, his presence might seem less obtrusive.

Drysdale started to observe Martin. He looked familiar for some reason. Just as Martin prepared to make his move, Drysdale moved a stool closer. 'Excuse me, are you from the States?'

Martin turned around. 'Why . . . yes.'

'Let me buy you a drink, Steve Drysdale's my name.'

'That's very kind of you, Steve, but I really must get a move on. I'm expected for dinner and . . .'

'Oh, come on, just a short one. No one is ever on time in Santo Domingo. Bartender! Another drink for the gentleman here.'

Before Martin could say anything, another glass filled high with ice and rum was put in front of him, a bottle of Coca-Cola beside it.

'So what is your name?' Drysdale inquired.

'Martin. James Martin.'

'You traveling through? On business?'

'No. I'm . . . I'm on holiday.'

'Strange time to come on holiday. This country is about to explode.'

'Well, there were some cheap flights so I figured I would take advantage . . . What do you do?'

'I'm with the US Embassy. Consular section.'

Somehow, Drysdale didn't strike Martin as the type one would find stamping visas. 'You all must be pretty concerned about this kidnapping.'

'We sure are. Nobody seems to have much information on this group that claims it, FART.'

'Do you think it poses a threat to other Americans here, like myself?'

'Hard to say. All we know is that it seems to be operating independently of the other main guerrilla organization here, the ELD. So its actions are hard to anticipate.' Drysdale suddenly realized that he was probably saying too much and turned the questions back on Martin. 'So what is your line of business?'

'I'm . . . I'm in computers.'

'Is that right?'

'Yeah. Listen, Steve, thanks for the drink. But I really must be off.' He took out his wallet to pay his tab. 'Pleasure to meet you, maybe I'll catch you in here again sometime.'

Drysdale kept looking in Martin's direction as he walked out of the swinging doors. He was sure that he had seen him before. He also seemed very nervous for someone on vacation. At that moment, all heads in the lounge turned as the doors swung open again and in walked Jane Winter, followed by her entourage.

10

'They won't settle for ten million? They want thirty?!' Brian Thorpe was absolutely aghast. 'We have offered them one of the highest ransoms ever paid in Central America and those Farts want three times as much. This is ridiculous, Tom.'

They had both just finished breakfast when the anonymous call was received. Tom Cross had returned to Thorpe's room bearing the bad news which he had picked up in the men's room.

'We have obviously been too easy on them, Tom. There is no way we can justify a higher offer. Write back saying that ten million is final and if that isn't bloody enough we are going to flush their next reply down the bloody toilet.'

'What if they know that Clark is covered for over twenty million?'

'They are not supposed to know . . . unless it's an inside job and the whole thing is a fraud. I'm beginning to have my doubts. If it wasn't for what Teresa told me I . . .'

'You mean you actually . . .'

'I just can't imagine a small band of hungry revolutionaries not settling for ten million, Tom. I really can't. I don't care how much training this character Carlos is supposed to have had in Libya. Something is not right.'

'Maybe they are not just a hungry band of revolutionaries. Perhaps they are a well-sustained organization. They do seem to have excellent intelligence capabilities.'

'Too excellent. You know what that girl Teresa told me? That their leader Carlos is a pimp. Can you believe that, a bloody pimp!' Thorpe kept walking around the room in an almost deranged fashion.

'That's not so unusual, Brian. Remember that case in New York when Libyan agents approached that small-time racketeer in Harlem; he was also involved in prostitution, if I recall, or illegal gambling or both. They wanted him to form a Black Muslim terrorist group.' Cross sat calmly at the foot of the unmade bed.

'I'll bet you anything that if he had kidnapped anybody he would have settled for ten million.' Thorpe helped himself to a bottle of fruit juice from the refrigerator.

'Not necessarily, if the Libyans or whoever controlled him had their reasons for wanting a higher payment, or for the case to drag out. Maybe these FART people or whoever is behind them may want to play this kidnapping for political gain. It's not worth it to them to lose the attention they are getting for less than twenty or thirty million, if only because they are an upstart group. You were with me down in the lounge last night when that American media star sauntered in. The Dominican Republic is in the international headlines for possibly the first time since the Americans landed twenty years ago.'

'Well, if that's the case, Tom, we will just have to find out more about this FART.' Thorpe finished his bottle with the third swig. 'See if the police or the Americans have anything new. I'll see what I can find out through my own channels.' He put down the bottle, picked up the phone and dialed Teresa's office number.

During his drive out to the safe house that day, Martin pondered about all the talent that must lie unrecognized in the Dominican Republic. For a nation its size, this country had produced its share of gifted and energetic individuals. America's currently most sought-after baseball star, Fernando Valenzuela, who had set a new world record for home runs, was Dominican born. El merengue, the Latin dance which was the hottest rave in New York's discotheques, was a Dominican creation. It was popularized by the Dominican Republic's longest surviving dictator, Rafael Trujillo who ran the country like his private estate all during the 1950s until he met his death in a bloody ambush planned by his political enemies assisted, so rumor has it, by the CIA.

It is told that during a formal ceremony to sign a peace treaty with neighboring Haiti following a brief border war, Trujillo felt so pleased that he ordered his military hand to strike up a merengue. He led the dance with the sixteen-year-old daughter of one of his ministers, holding her and twirling her to the hard fast beat for more than three hours in front of all the assembled dignitaries. He later married her.

A bodyguard of Trujillo's, Porfirio Rubirosa, rose to become one of the twentieth century's most accomplished international playboys. He seduced and married two of the richest women in the world at the time, Barbara Hutton and Doris Duke. One of the American mega-heiresses is known to have said of Rubirosa that 'the moment he walks into a room I feel as if I've just been hit over the head.' He died in a fatal car accident in the South of France.

These thoughts came back to Martin as he observed Carlos fitting together his bomb of dynamite and butane gas. He had strapped five sticks of explosive to the orange tank containing eighty cubic feet of pressurized gas. He was now fitting the concoction into the spare wheel underneath the trunk of a '69

Chevrolet which Luis had managed to 'borrow'. The location for the bomb had the added advantage of being right above the fuel tank.

'I tell you, *amigo*, with this we shatter every window in the center of Santo Domingo.' He finished fastening the straps to make sure that the bomb would hold down tightly. All that remained to be done was fix on the detonator fuse made of an electric battery, timer watch and blasting cap. The timer would be wound up for the minutes it would take Carlos to clear the plaza. When it stopped, an electric current would run through the attached battery which, in turn, would set off the blasting cap and fuse the dynamite.

Earlier, Martin had observed John Clark and Nora frolicking around in the natural stream that ran through the back of the house. The presence of *Tres* standing nearby with his shotgun didn't seem to faze him in the least. Martin wondered if Clark wasn't becoming a male Patty Hearst, who fell in love with her abductors, engaging in bisexual sex with them and eventually becoming a participant in their 'military operations'. Psychiatrists coined the term 'Stockholm Syndrome' to describe the repeated phenomenon in which hostages develop a sense of mutual identification with their captors. It was named for a case in which the female employee of a Stockholm bank, held by a group of bank robbers, voluntarily engaged in sexual intercourse with one of them inside a vault. Dominican Syndrome more like, Martin thought.

Carlos wiped his hands with a greasy rag, his exposed torso gleaming with sweat. 'Who will drive with me into the plaza tonight?'

Carlos had volunteered to deliver the bomb. But somebody had to go with him to drive the getaway car. Luis was already being asked to do too much, *Cinco* was unreliable and at least two had to remain in the safe house with Clark and Nora at all times, eliminating *Dos* and *Tres*. This only left Martin. 'I guess I'll have to do it.'

That afternoon, Brian Thorpe lay in his hotel bed with Teresa. She didn't have much new information, but she was giving him something else. Now he relaxed with a cigarette, his right arm wrapped around her warm naked body, his hand caressing her nicely rounded bottom. 'So *you* haven't found anything new, and neither the police nor the American Embassy have anything either.'

'Only one small thing, Brian.' She felt around his muscular stomach, deciding to tell him the bit that she knew. 'FART is passing on messages through a house of prostitution.'

'Which one? That's a rather widespread industry here.'

'I don't know.'

'At least you have more than the police.'

'Have you had any further communication with FART?'

'They rejected our offer.'

'For how much?'

'I can only tell you that they are now asking thirty million.' Thorpe squeezed her body towards him, pressing his lips against hers as his thigh felt the moisture between her legs.

Martin and Carlos were pushing the '69 Chevy towards the Chase Manhattan Bank building just off the Plaza de la Catedral. The car had sputtered to a dead stop about a block away, as if the engine, sensing its fate, had decided to die out on its own before being blown to pieces.

'Just half a block more, *amigo*,' Carlos gasped.

'We don't want to get too close, there are bound to be security guards inside who could see us.' But Martin had to admit that Carlos had been right. It was an hour past midnight and the plaza was completely dark and deserted. There were no lights anywhere, except for those which shone from the inside of the cathedral and a couple of lit windows, in the Chase building, which they had now reached at last.

Carlos got into the car to apply the handbrake, emerging again with the detonator fuse. He set the timer for fifteen minutes, lit his small flashlight and started to fasten on the mechanism. Martin turned to head for the Ford Fiesta he had parked behind the cathedral on the far side of the square when he heard Carlos whisper '*Carajo!*'

'What's the matter?'

'The fuse does not work.'

'What do you mean?'

'The timer doesn't run.'

'What the hell are we going to do now? How the hell are we going to move this thing? Can't you make it work again?'

'I don't know how. The catch is dead.'

'Oh for God's sake, Carlos, how . . .'

'There is only one thing we can do, *amigo*.' Carlos took a stick of dynamite from the bouquet strapped to the gas tank. He took out a penknife from the hip pocket of his jeans, and cut open the top of the thin cylindrical container. He then placed his foot on the bumper, pulled out a shoelace from his sneaker and fixed it to the dynamite wrapped in plastic which dropped out of the cylinder.

'Carlos, what are you going to do? Carlos?' Martin started to walk backwards.

Carlos didn't answer. He just unscrewed the cap from the petrol tank, dipped in the shoelace that hung from the package of dynamite and then dropped the dynamite into the petrol tank. He set a match to the hanging shoelace and started to run.

Martin was already well ahead of him. He noticed a deep stone archway in one of the old buildings flanking the plaza and dove inside. Just as he heard the exploding fuel tank, Carlos flew in on top of him. In a split second there was a deafening second explosion, infinitely louder than the first. The ground shook, making it difficult for Martin to keep his head down. Even with his eyes closed he could sense the flash of light that illuminated the plaza as a mushroom cloud of burning gas and petrol was released into the atmosphere.

Flaming debris and sharded glass fell everywhere. When he looked up, Martin could recognize a burning tire on the sidewalk a few feet from them. Another large piece of flaming metal crashed down, either the hood or the roof. He tried to move but Carlos was heavily on top of him, seemingly shellshocked.

'You goddam fucking idiot, you could have had us both killed. This place is going to be crawling with army and police in a minute.' Carlos just kept lying on top, speechless. 'What the hell are we going to tell them when they find us here, for the second time, on top of each other? That we're gay?'

Carlos sat up and looked around. Bits of flaming metal and splintered glass still showered down from the heavens. He pointed towards the cathedral. 'In there, I know the priest who gives Mass at night. He is for the revolution. Come.'

They got up and peered out of the archway. The car was a fireball. Martin and Carlos picked their way across the plaza through the sea of broken glass and flaming wreckage to the back entrance of the cathedral. Martin realized that they were in front of Columbus's tomb; a three-layered mausoleum, with wooden edges encrusted in plated gold and surrounded by innumerable rows of lit candles mountainous with melted wax. It gave the appearance of a fallen chandelier.

They crept beyond the tomb, spotting the altar at the far end of the cathedral. The priest had his back to them as he faced a primitive image of the crucifixion engraved in mosaics on the bare stone wall. He was going through the rites of the Eucharist. Only one other hunched-up, solitary figure was there, kneeling in prayer. Neither seemed to have been affected in the least by the explosion which still reverberated in Martin and Carlos's ears. A guttural sound suddenly echoed throughout the cathedral, making both of them jump. In spite of their semi-deafened states, the acoustics inside were formidable. When a second sound bounced up, they realized that it was the worshipper clearing her throat.

Carlos pointed to an empty confessional. 'You go hide there, I will speak to the priest.'

As he sat behind the velvet curtain, Martin's body kept trembling. The hollowness in his ears was suddenly pierced by the sound of sirens approaching the plaza. The next moment they were passing right by, followed by the heavy rumbling of military vehicles. Cars and trucks were now screeching to a halt, orders being barked out. Just then, Carlos peered inside the confessional as he flung open the curtain. He was attired as an altar boy. He pushed a dark garment on to Martin's lap. 'Here, put this on.' It was a cassock. Martin pulled it over his head, buttoning the top. It fitted snugly over his shirt and trousers. 'You go there.' Carlos pointed towards the hunched figure. 'Next to the old lady. Kneel down and pretend you are praying.'

'I don't think I'll need to pretend.'

'I will stand at the altar next to the Padre.'

Martin rushed down the aisle behind Carlos to take his assigned place. Carlos reached the altar as the priest began Communion. No sooner had he raised the cup, '*Esta es mi sangre*,' than a loud banging was heard at the cathedral's front door. The priest took the necessary time to finish the ritual, stepped off the altar and disappeared towards the side. The sound of heavy bolts unfastening could be heard, and then some gruff voices.

Several uniformed men followed the priest inside. 'As you can see,' he said, 'there is nobody here except for the *señora* –' the old lady's meditation remained uninterrupted '– and two of my brothers.'

'We just needed to make sure, Padre,' the mustachioed lieutenant explained. 'A security guard at the bank says he saw two figures running from the explosion in this direction.'

'I assure you that nobody has come in here. Now, if you don't mind I would like to get back to my service.'

'Very good, Padre, but isn't it a bit late to be giving Mass?'

'Ah well, you see, *Teniente*, that old lady praying there, communicating so deeply with God, she has lost all of her family. I give a special Mass once a week only for her so that she may pray for all of their souls. And since she has nobody to pray with, one of our brothers always prays with her. She had a large family.'

'*Entiendo. Buenas noches, Padre.*'

'*Vaya con Dios.*'

It was still dark when the telephone rang in Brian Thorpe's room. He became instantly alert as he picked up the receiver and heard the tape recording of a muffled voice speaking in accented English: 'At one hundred hours this morning, five kilos of plastic explosive were detonated inside a 1969 Chevrolet automobile outside the central offices of the Chase Manhattan Bank. The Workers' Revolutionary Armed

Forces claims sole responsibility for this action which strikes at the heart of Yankee capitalist multinational imperialism, its lackeys and pernicious conspiracies against the oppressed people of the Dominican Republic and everywhere warriors of socialism fight and die daily for their freedom and dignity . . . If our demand for thirty million dollars is not met within forty-eight hours from the time of this telephone message, the next explosion will be a bullet through John Clark's head. We expect your reply in the usual place.' The line went dead.

There was a knock on the door. Thorpe opened it to let in Tom Cross. 'I just received a call . . .'

'Me too.' Thorpe disappeared into the bathroom to splash some cold water on his face.

'There was also this note outside my door.'

Thorpe came back out of the bathroom and took the piece of paper. It was a photocopy of John Clark's New York driver's licence.

'There was also this.' Cross produced a small bottle. 'It's a urine sample. To prove that he is still alive.'

'How considerate.'

'Suppose anyone was killed in that bombing? The windows in my room shook.'

'I felt it too. Obviously one hell of a loud fart.' Thorpe allowed the witticism to hang as he slipped into a pair of trousers. 'Suggest we get over there and have a look.'

Dawn was starting to break as the two ransom negotiators walked across the plaza. Fire trucks had doused the flames, but military vehicles still blocked off the area around the smouldering wreckage. Helmeted police and soldiers milled about as clean-up crews began the arduous task of removing the smoking debris, splintered glass and other rubble that lay strewn along the avenida. The smell of cordite, burned butane and petrol was still thick in the humid air. A light breeze blowing in from the bay only stirred up the stink still further.

Tom Cross went over to talk with the officer who seemed to be in charge of the clean-up operation. Thorpe inspected the upturned heap of corrugated metal which had once been a car. A gaping hole several feet in diameter offered a view into the interior of the Chase building. They were not the only outside observers. Jane Winter and her television team were also there, covering the scene together with several other journalists and photographers, both local and foreign.

Thorpe stood scratching his head as Cross walked back over to him. 'The Captain tells me that there were no serious casualties. One of the bank's security guards was cut by flying glass.'

'I don't think it was five kilos of plastic explosive, Tom. Half this side of the building would have collapsed and there would be absolutely nothing left of the car.' During his six-month tour of duty in Northern Ireland, Thorpe had seen many Semtex bombings. 'The impact of the explosion was considerable.' He looked around at the rows of shattered windows throughout the Chase building and elsewhere in the plaza. 'But I would say that the explosion itself was of medium intensity. There is indeed nothing left of the rear half of the car where the bomb obviously was placed. But the front part, as you can see, was consumed mostly by fire. Look, you can still see traces of the engine. I would say that it was either a moderate amount of TNT or dynamite with an enhancer, such as pressurized gas. I do smell butane in the air, don't you, Tom?'

'So what do you think that means?'

'What I have suspected all along. That FART is trying to make itself look bigger than it actually is.

One would imagine that a group with Libyan connections would have access to high-explosive plastic like Semtex or C-4. I'm convinced that neither was used in this operation, certainly not five kilos.'

'May have been a smaller amount. Besides, try explaining that to them.' Cross pointed towards the American television team, now in the process of filming Jane Winter doing her piece to camera: 'It's called the F-A-R-T, which in Spanish stands for Revolutionary Armed Front of the Workers. It is holding hostage an American businessman. With this latest gust in the revolutionary hurricane sweeping the Dominican Republic where US Marines landed twenty years ago, the FART tells the world that it means business ... this is Jane Winter for *NBN Evening News* in Santo Domingo.'

Comandante Nueve had been quite busy over the past day receiving and debriefing the first group of his guerrillas to return from training in Nicaragua, twenty in all. Some forty more were expected back in the next several days. He was satisfied that their re-entry into the Dominican Republic was going undetected. They would be subdivided into small groups and deployed in various safe houses which were being arranged throughout the city.

They all looked fit, hungry for action and honed in the latest techniques of rural and urban guerrilla insurgency. Veteran instructors from Cuba, the PLO, Libya and an assortment of international terrorist networks had schooled them expertly in the black arts of armed subversion. Each of them now knew how to destroy an entire office block using only a few pounds of plastic explosive; how to handle anti-tank and anti-aircraft weapons; how to cut off the electricity supply to an entire city; how to assemble and disassemble machine guns and automatic rifles; how to endure torture and interrogation, manage secret communications and take on vastly superior forces using surprise-tactics.

Most importantly, they had developed the discipline and endurance to put their knowledge into practice. These men would be the spearhead of the upcoming offensive code-named 'Plan Zero', which *Comandante Nueve* would put into operation the moment those weapons Castro had been promising arrived.

But he was now back on the problem of FART. News of the bombing outside the Chase Manhattan Bank had reminded him of something that he wished he could simply forget about. Teresa and *Comandante Cuatro* once again sat before *Nueve* in his underground command bunker as he went over freshly developed photographs of the explosion's aftermath, taken by an ELD agent working as a news photographer.

'This fireworks display is typical of amateurs.' His cement complexion seemed grayer than ever in the harsh white light of his battery-operated interrogation lamp. 'But somebody must be assisting them in that kidnapping. Of that I am convinced.'

'You know that an American TV news team was covering the scene this morning,' *Comandante Cuatro* said, 'building up FART as the main revolutionary group in the Dominican Republic.'

Comandante Nueve could barely contain his rage.' So what else have you found out?'

'We know that they are passing messages through Casa Las Familias. The group is communicating through there. We have been watching the place. But until now, none of them have turned up.'

Comandante Nueve turned to Teresa. 'And what have you found out from those ransom negotiators? I hope that you have not been fucking with that *Ingles* for pleasure.'

Teresa had learned to ignore *Nueve*'s contempt for

anything that approached human happiness. She respected him and his mission. But their brief moments together were never anything more than sexual releases. 'They are seriously negotiating a ransom. FART rejected an offer which they made for Clark, how much I don't know. But FART is now asking thirty million.'

'Thirty million!' *Comandante Nueve* was shocked. 'Those clowns are asking thirty million? Rejecting an offer? That is incredible! It is preposterous!' He turned again on *Cuatro*. 'Double the surveillance on that *Casa de Putas*. When whoever it is that's passing the messages turns up, have him followed.'

'We really should answer them as soon as possible, Brian.' Thorpe and Cross were having a late breakfast of bacon and scrambled eggs by the poolside of their hotel. A tall palm tree shaded their table from the heat of the morning sun.

'I realize, Tom.' Thorpe took a mouthful of his scrambled eggs. 'I think at this point a meeting with FART's fearless leader is in order.'

'You mean face-to-face negotiations? What kind of offer are you suggesting we make?'

'Nothing more than what we have offered already.'

'I think it might be wise to go above the ten million.'

'And encourage them to set off more bombs? The poor buggers will run out of dynamite.'

'Remember that Puerto Rican nationalist group in the United States? They were setting off dynamite charges of an even lower grade than this one. When the FBI rounded them up in Chicago, they were well advanced in plans to kidnap President Reagan's son.'

'They didn't get around to doing it, did they?'

'This is not the United States is it, Brian? The FART are obviously not feeling much police pressure or they would not have set off that bomb last night – dynamite, Semtex or whatever. You saw that smashing American newswoman, FART is getting big international publicity. They would have every reason to hold out for a high price on John Clark. He is becoming very valuable to them. They may even decide to stick the political demands back on. Frankly, Brian, I think the longer this drags out, the harder it's going to be to get him out. Let's just give them an offer they can't refuse now.'

'Ten million is high enough. I may possibly intimate in my message that we will consider withdrawing our offer altogether if they don't agree to a face-to-face meeting between myself and Carlos.'

'You are playing with this man's life, Brian.' Tom Cross was becoming impatient with Thorpe's smugness. 'Do you realize the media hype they will get if they kill Clark? Every other company in the Dominican Republic would be paying them millions in protection money.'

'Calm down, Tom.' Thorpe had respect for Cross's intellect. He accepted his cautious views as a necessary balance to his own daredevil instincts. But he also knew from experience that terrorists did not dispose of their hostages all that easily, and he did not see why FART should be any different. Besides, he had a card to play which Cross did not yet know about. 'Bear in mind that they positioned and timed last night's bomb to minimize casualties. Furthermore, I have some information that might be of interest to them.'

'Such as what?'

'They may not be feeling much pressure from the police. But the ELD has found the location of FART's message drop. A brothel, apparently.'

Martin closed the door behind him as he entered his room. It was just before lunch. The note from Thorpe and Cross had been in the usual place. He pulled it from the inside pocket of his jacket and tore open the envelope. It read:

> We made a first-hand inspection of your bomb damage this morning. Any further terrorist actions on your part could seriously jeopardize the course of our negotiations. In order to consider further the payment of a ransom for Mr Jonathan Clark III, we must have (a) current and direct proof that he is still alive – via a telephone conversation with him and (b) you must agree to a face-to-face meeting between ourselves and designated representatives of FART leadership.
>
> We may be able to settle our offer of ten million US dollars if these conditions are met. But your demand of thirty million is entirely unrealistic. A marginal increase over our current offer is the very most that could possibly be negotiated.
>
> It may interest you to know that certain sources here have informed us of a facility which you are using for your communications. It is, according to these sources, a brothel. We would be willing to inform you further about this in a meeting with your representatives.

Martin read and re-read the last paragraph, until the full ramifications had sunk in. Part of their operation had been uncovered and was being watched. But by whom? It could not be the police. He was wondering out loud to himself who the hell else it could be when there came a frantic knocking at the door.

'Who is it?'

'*Soy yo.*' It was Graciela.

He quickly opened the door and she rushed inside. She was in a highly agitated state, her face tear-streaked. 'They are watching Las Familias. Pepita, one of the girls, told me this morning not to go there, someone from the ELD has been asking questions. Oh, Martin, I'm so frightened, I'm so scared.'

Martin held her by the shoulders. 'How do you know it's the ELD?'

'The barman recognized this man as *un jefe del distrito*. He beat up Pepita to get information from her.'

Martin felt as if he had been hit by a sudden gust of freezing wind. 'Have you warned off Luis?' Graciela's expression was blank. 'Answer me, have you warned off Luis?' He shook her.

Tears started streaming down her cheeks. 'No.'

'Oh, shit.' Luis would be in the process of delivering the fresh photographs of Clark, just about now.

Diagonally across the pot-holed street from Casa Las Familias, a man sat inside a blue Ford, chainsmoking his black tobacco cigarettes. He was a member of the *Comandos Informativos*, the intelligence-gathering arm of the ELD. They were kept entirely apart from the 'military groups', or 'action cells', their function consisting exclusively of surveying and gathering information on potential targets for terrorist assault.

Another man of the *Comando*, who had been sitting discreetly inside Casa Las Familias, walked out of the house and over to the car.

'It's him. His name is Luis. He just left an envelope with the barman.'

The man had just got in and shut the car door, when the slender figure of Luis, in a white, short-sleeved office shirt, emerged through the front gate.

They started the engine as he walked towards his car. When Luis took off, they followed.

Herbert Lopwitz was in his private study, on the phone with Colonel Ventura in Santo Domingo. '. . . Come on, Colonel, I hardly think that a cut-up security guard constitutes bloodshed . . . All right, it's a deal, you get the apartment in Miami plus a hundred thousand dollars of the ransom . . . Agreed, I'll tell my man to play down the publicity . . . I know there is pressure on you . . . Look, Colonel, I'm not the one you should be telling about generals on your back, tell that to the ransom negotiators . . .'

Lopwitz hung up and checked the papers in the open briefcase in front of him. The time had come to lay down arrangements for laundering the ransom money. One way or another, there would soon be a settlement to the kidnapping. Several new bank accounts would have to be opened as well as a network of offshore companies to engineer the bail-out loan for Sanitex Equipment and raise additional funds for the operation, if necessary. He had found the right banker to do it, a man adept at international money-laundering, used regularly by intelligence agencies, arms traffickers, drug dealers and the like. He had a private meeting arranged with him for tomorrow.

It was time for Lopwitz to catch his plane. He snapped shut his briefcase and reached for the overnight bag. The thought of calling Martin occurred to him, but he was not sure that he wanted to tell him about the pressures building up, not just yet. It could discourage him from holding out for the full twenty million. He would call him after talking again with Ventura once he was in Panama.

11

Martin crashed into the water, head first, and swam at full stretch up and down the length of the pool. Carlos had practically had a fit when he told him what was going on. If Luis was being tailed, the ELD would be getting led to the safe house at this very moment. Or worse yet, Luis might be captured and in the process of a brutal interrogation. Carlos was going to call him back in an hour.

His mind kept turning as he free-styled for several more lengths. Martin had tried calling Lopwitz in New York, only to be told by his secretary that the 'Acting Chairman' had left on a brief business trip and would he like to leave a message? He had then tried his private number, only to get the machine.

They should be settling for whatever they could get at this point. Setting up the direct meeting which the ransom negotiators required with Carlos was now complicated, if not downright impossible. After reaching the shallow end of his fifteenth lap, Martin pulled himself out of the water and lay down on a lounger to dry off in the sun.

He had just shut his eyes when he felt a shadow fall on him. He rolled them open again to see Jane Winter skimpily clad in a plain white bikini. 'Hi Martin,' she said, 'you're a pretty good swimmer.'

'Oh my God!' Martin could barely contain his exclamation to a loud whisper. Just three months ago, Jane Winter had spent an afternoon at his office consulting him on material for a documentary which she was preparing on international terrorism. In their last communication he had rudely slammed down the phone when she turned him down for a date. Now she was perhaps the last person that he needed to see.

Away from the poolside, sitting at a table near the snack bar, wearing dark glasses, was Steven Drysdale. He had just finished lunching with Jane Winter and from what Jane had told him Drysdale now knew who Martin was.

'I regret to inform you, gentlemen, that, as I warned you might occur, my department is under pressure from our military superiors to move more strongly on this kidnapping and cut off any private negotiations which may be in progress with FART to pay a ransom for John Clark.'

Brian Thorpe and Tom Cross had received a call from Colonel Ventura summoning them urgently to his office. The ransom negotiators now sat before him.

'Colonel.' Thorpe tried to appeal to reason. 'If we are forced to settle now, we will be giving FART much more money than they would otherwise get. Do you want an even stronger terrorist group around to carry out more kidnappings in future?'

'Things are moving out of my control, Mr Thorpe.' Colonel Ventura sat forward, cupping his hands on the desk in front of him. 'Two generals came to see me this morning. They want me to stop all negotiations with FART right now. As police chief of Santo Domingo, I can only act with limited authority. As you may know, the police in this country are a branch of the armed forces. The most that I can give you is twenty-four hours more in which to conclude your negotiations.'

As he turned his car for the last stretch of road into the Plantacion de Arguelles, Luis came to a slow stop. Now he *knew* he was being followed. That same light-blue Ford had followed all his twists and turns as he wound his way up into the mountains.

He had turned off into the dirt road leading to the final stretch when the fearful realization had become too pressing to ignore. He got out and hid behind a thick tree. The rumbling of another car engine was definitely audible, moving slowly over the holes and bumps and mud-puddles. Peering through the thick foliage, Luis could just about make out the silver gleam of the front bumper. It moved closer and there was no doubt. It was the light-blue Ford.

Martin was back in his hotel room on the phone to Carlos, who had just spoken with Luis. 'Carlos . . . getting like this is not going to help matters . . . Look, will you please calm down, the fact of the matter is that we don't know what the ELD are going to do . . . yes, I realize what mean sons of bitches they are . . . look, Carlos, listen, will you just listen, this is what I'm going to do . . .'

After finishing his conversation, Martin picked up his notebook and looked up the number for Major Otero at police headquarters. 'I know of some excellent bodyguards,' was the first thing the fly-swatting head of police intelligence had told Martin on the morning in which he had gone to see him.

The two ransom negotiators were now at the US Embassy, talking to Frank Burns.

'I'm sorry, you guys.' Burns reclined sideways in his chair, legs stretched out, clicking and unclicking a US government-issue ballpoint pen. 'There is simply nothing we can do.'

After seeing Ventura, Thorpe had requested an urgent meeting with the American Ambassador, who had referred him to the Chargé d'Affaires, who had referred him back to the Regional Security Officer – whom Thorpe had previously seen. He was trying to convince the US Embassy to apply pressure on the Dominican government to allow the ransom negotiations to continue unhindered. Since Clark was a US citizen, it was a matter which should concern them, Thorpe had thought, sensibly enough.

'It is our policy not to get involved in private ransom negotiations. Official US policy is not to negotiate with terrorists, period. If such matters are a purely private or corporate concern, we don't interfere. But there is no way that we are going to influence the government here, to make it easier for you to ransom Clark. The Ambassador is quite adamant on that.'

They had walked the few blocks between the hotel and the US Embassy. But in the middle of a Caribbean afternoon, even a short walk was a hot one. They were tieless, their shirts soaked through with perspiration. Thorpe mopped his forehead with a handkerchief, his normally light complexion radiating redness.

'But, Mr Burns, you don't seem to get my point. By cutting off negotiations, all that is effectively being done is forcing us to pay a higher ransom than we might otherwise be able to negotiate for Clark. We may have to pay up his entire coverage. This is clearly not in the interests of the insurance company, or of the government's, or yours. It's your citizens who are going to be targets of future kidnappings as FART grows bigger and thinks it's on to a good thing.'

'I understand your argument, Brian, but we just can't get involved. You say that you will have to pay a higher ransom for Clark than you otherwise would. But that's because the Chief of Police is privately leaving you some leeway to finish your job. It has nothing to do with the official policy of the government which is that you should not be paying a ransom at all.' Burns pulled in his legs, sitting up straight and leaning forward. 'I mean, how does it make us look if we go ask the President or the Interior Minister to allow your negotiations to progress? What kind of position would that put us in next time we ask the government to crack down on terrorist activity or to extradite a drug dealer or something? Try looking at it from our perspective.'

'As I understand it, Frank, it's not so much the government as the military who are pressuring the police to cut off negotiations. Colonel Ventura told me that two generals had been in to see him this morning.'

'Well, if it's an army matter then you should talk to our military attaché.'

Comandante Nueve was in his underground bunker, speaking on the radio telephone with his *informativos*. The men had spotted two armed guards, one of whom looked like Carlos. He ordered them to remain on watch and hooked the receiver back. Plantacion de Arguelles, he thought to himself ... now that he recalled, he knew of the owner. Federico de Arguelles was the son of a prominent Dominican landowning family. He had made a personal fortune in drug dealing and had gone to live in Florida. Was it just possible that the drug mafia had staged this kidnapping for some obscure reason of their own, fronting it through FART?

Comandante Nueve had some important drug-trafficking connections. They did him many favors and paid substantial contributions to his movement through a secret ELD account in Panama, as much or more than the Cubans gave. In return, the ELD would provide such services as protecting their high-grade marijuana fields or guarding clandestine air-strips which served as refueling stops for planes ferrying cocaine between Colombia and the United States.

But if they were involved in this kidnapping, why would they be using FART? And how could they not have cleared it with him? It didn't make any sense. He would call his own contact in Miami to see if he could talk with Arguelles to find out what this was all about. It might also be time to start finding out a few things about the Sanitex Equipment Corporation. *Comandante Nueve* reached back for his phone.

Martin had started smoking again after nearly a year. When he had finished trying to calm down the near-hysterical Carlos he had called a special protection service which Major Otero had recommended. A man with a gruff voice identifying himself over the telephone as '*El Jefe*' had agreed to meet him in the hotel at midnight along with a dozen of his best men. When Martin told him that the job involved guarding a country estate against a possible attack by the ELD, *El Jefe* said that they would come armed with automatic rifles, machine guns and grenades. Now he was out of cigarettes.

At the reception desk, Martin was directed to the bar. Inside the smoky cocktail lounge, a merengue band was striking up with *Brunilda*, loudly enough to make him shout his order to the barman. While preparing to make a quick exit, Martin felt a soft hand taking his arm and that feminine, throaty, mildly Southern voice, cooing in his ear.

'You were supposed to call me earlier, mystery man, what happened to you?'

'Oh, Jane, sorry, I've . . . I've been kind of busy. I . . . I was going to call you later.'

When they talked after her surprise appearance at the pool, Jane had suggested that they get together for dinner. Martin would have never dreamt in his wildest nightmares that he would be trying to get out of a dinner date with Jane Winter, but he had put her off, saying that he would call her later. Tragically, the circumstances were not propitious for the company of one of the most thorough research journalists and most aggressive newswomen in American television, however blonde and beautiful.

'I'm here with my crew; how would you like to join us for a drink?'

'I'd really love to, Jane, but I've got all this work to do and I really should . . .'

'Oh, come on, Martin, what are you doing that's so important, organizing a terrorist conspiracy?' She stroked back her long blonde hair.

Martin said nothing.

'Now don't be such a spoilsport.' Locking her arm into his, she pulled him along.

The band was winding down as Jane introduced Martin around her table to cameraman Jack Haines, sound technician Nick Potowsky and production assistant Linda Shaeffer as a 'terrorism expert'. They were impressed. Martin only wished he could crawl under a chair and hide.

Jane's words were overheard just a couple of tables away where Brian Thorpe and Tom Cross sat drinking gin and tonics, after their harrowing afternoon. They had actually waited almost an hour to get into see the military attaché, only to extract some vague promise from the US army's Lieutenant-Colonel that he would inquire as to whether somebody in the the Dominican high command would be willing to meet with them.

'Did you hear that, Brian? A terrorism expert. What do you suppose he's doing with them?' Cross sipped his drink.

'God knows, probably some pundit who managed to crawl into her bed.' Thorpe sat back, passing his cool glass over his forehead.

'It may be interesting to hear what he has to say.'

'I doubt if he has anything that we don't already know.'

A waiter served a tray full of daquiris around Jane Winter's table. She popped a handful of cashew nuts into her mouth and crossed her legs to reveal a very sexy pair of thighs. 'So, Martin, what do you think about this group FART – isn't the name a scream? We were filming this morning at the place where they set off that bomb.'

'It was one helluva fart,' interjected the cameraman.

'Oh, shut up, Jack. Now tell me, what do you think, Martin, is it really Libyan-trained and all that? What would the Libyans be doing here?'

Martin felt he should make the best of the situation. 'Well, actually, Jane, there has been a developing pattern of Libyan activity in the region recently. When we invaded Grenada, for example, significant stores of Libyan arms, ammunition and other military material were found on the island. There are also reports of groups of Libyan instructors operating in Nicaragua. Libya has been supplying arms to the Sandinistas, too.'

Jane studied him. She had found Martin interesting from the first time that she met him but had been too busy back in Washington to deal with his advances, as persistent as they were. Now he looked so tan and fit. It would definitely have to happen; especially in view of what she had been asked to do by Drysdale.

'Come on, Martin, let's have a dance.'

Jumping at the chance to avoid further questioning, Martin led her on to the crowded dance floor, as the band started up a slow, romantic merengue.

Tres was patroling the grounds around the house as Carlos had ordered him to do. He carried the shotgun, with both barrels loaded, and a flashlight. The sun had gone down just under an hour ago, and the night birds and insects were in full cry.

Wearing his camouflaged T-shirt, *Tres* was alert and dead serious about his task. He had been told that they were being watched and felt thrilled with the anticipation of real action, not really caring with whom or why.

Something rustled in one of the bushes. *Tres* immediately turned his flashlight in the direction of the noise, knowing that there weren't any large animals around these parts, unless it was some stray dog. The beam of light moved just in time for his eye to catch sight of what was definitely the back of a human figure scurrying for cover into a large clump of tall grass. He released the safety catch and aimed the shotgun. '*Detengase, quien va ahi*,' he yelled.

No sooner had he finished than he heard the distinct crack of revolver shots. They were being fired from some bushes further behind. A bullet came close and he crouched, instinctively, firing one of his barrels in the direction of the shots. There was a cry of pain. Next, he turned the gun back on the figure he had first seen, who was now poised to make a run for it. '*Quieto!*' shouted *Tres*.

Following their dance, Martin finally managed to excuse himself gracefully, suggesting to Jane Winter that they get together for dinner some other night. But he had not been back in his room for an hour before the door sounded and Martin found her inviting herself in.

They were now rolling around his bed. She had his shirt off and was working her hand into his trousers, wanting a touch of what had felt so good rubbing up to her on the dance floor. He had unhooked her bra, stroking her breasts before he started to feel his way up her warm thigh. His fingers had discovered the gathering wetness when the phone rang.

Martin struggled to untangle himself. Carlos was on the other end, rattling away about the shoot-out and not allowing Martin to get a word in edgeways, which in view of the circumstances was just as well. When he heard, however, that a member of the ELD surveillance team had been taken prisoner Martin wanted to jump off the bed, letting out a loud gasp as Jane kept holding on to what made any sudden movement inadvisable.

Jane was in a passionate heat. But her professional curiosity was also aroused by what was becoming an intense exchange as Carlos suggested that they abandon the safe house. The trick of keeping Jane uninvolved and Carlos reassured seemed impossible. 'Listen . . . er . . . Carl. It's very hard for me to talk to you right now.' Martin thought of switching to Spanish, but Jane probably spoke it. So instead, he just kept saying, 'Carl! I have company, please understand that I have company with me. I can't talk right now. Hold back and don't move and I will be there very soon with what I promised I would bring you.' He had told Carlos earlier that he would be arriving with some well-armed bodyguards at some point during the night. But Carlos persisted in his monologue, accusing Martin of not caring if he and his entire group got slaughtered. The ELD could arrive in force at any moment and heaven knew how many more were already out there. Martin did not think that there could be any significant number in the immediate vicinity or they would have probably pounced by now and *Tres* would not still be alive – as he probably did not deserve to be. But communicating this with his manhood still in the firm grasp of NEN's ace reporter was one of the toughest challenges of his professional career.

Comandante Nueve was sitting in his bunker with one of his best and most trusted lieutenants, *Comandante Siete*, who had just re-entered the country from Nicaragua with another dozen trained guerrilla fighters. They were discussing the situation in Santo Domingo when a call came through from Miami. *Nueve*'s connection doubted that Arguelles had anything to do with the kidnapping. The owner did not even know that his house had been rented out recently.

Nueve filled in *Siete* on the preposterous kidnapping incident, but *Siete* switched the subject back to the latest techniques in demolitions which he had learned at the terrorist training camp in Nicaragua. He was eager to apply the knowledge. *Nueve* had stopped listening, though. His mind was running in circles. Someone had obviously rented the Arguelles house for FART. Who that was he could only guess right now. But how far could he trust whatever information came out of Miami? How could he be sure that the drug mafia was not in some way behind it? A spider web began to form in his mind; he imagined a conspiracy aimed at breaking his hold over the revolutionary movement in the Dominican Republic being hatched between Fidel Castro, who had not yet sent him his arms, and the drug barons, with some backhanded inspiration from the CIA. *Nueve*'s field telephone then rang. His chief of information and coordination for the Santo Domingo region, *Comandante Cuatro*, was on the other end with some disturbing news.

'Make sure that you get him to a doctor, I will handle this from here on.' When *Nueve* put down the phone he was fuming, only managing to control his temper because at least he was now certain about what needed to be done next. Not only were Carlos and FART undermining his pre-eminence as the Dominican Republic's revolutionary leader, but those clowns now held prisoner one of his *comandos informativos*.

The situation had become not only intolerable but a security risk as well. Whoever was behind this farce was going to be taught a lesson.

Comandante Nueve stood up behind his desk, looking directly at *Siete*. 'Get your men together. You are all going for a little firing practice tonight. Make your way to the Plantacion de Arguelles. Kill every single member of FART that you find, rescue my *comando informativo* and bring this John Clark back alive to me here. If anyone is going to bargain for hostages, it's going to be me!'

Miraculously, or so he thought, Martin had managed to conclude the telephone conversation with Carlos without disastrously arousing Jane's curiosity. A continuous mantra of 'I will get what we need to you soon, I will get what we need over there very soon,' had eventually succeeded in convincing Carlos not to do anything rash like fleeing the house. 'If you don't keep things as they are, I won't be able to get it over to you. The project would certainly end up dead then, wouldn't it, Carl?'

'What was all that about?' Jane had inquired as he put down the phone, visibly shaken.

'Oh, nothing, babe, just this guy back at the office who is all worked up about a deadline we have to meet on this report which I'm writing on the Dominican Republic. He just wants to go ahead and publish what we have now and I'm –'

'Don't insult my intelligence with this bullshit – and don't call me babe!' Jane straightened her skirt and tugged her unbuttoned blouse over her breasts.

'Look, Jane, if I was really doing something you are not supposed to know about, don't you think I would have asked you to leave the room? Or would you rather I hadn't let you in in the first place?' He had reached for a cigarette. No sooner did he have it lit than Jane took it and stubbed it out. She looked closely at him with half-closed eyes. 'Put out the light,' she said.

It was half-past midnight when the telephone rang again in Martin's room. They had both drifted off to sleep after making love. Martin picked up the phone, praying that it would not disturb Jane. *El Jefe*'s gruff voice was on the line from downstairs. He and his men were waiting in two Land Rovers in the hotel's parking lot.

'I'll be right down.' Martin quietly stepped out of the bed, grabbed for his jeans and the first shirt he could find, picked up a pair of sneakers and silently slipped out the door, confident that Jane hadn't woken up.

No sooner had the door clicked shut than Jane opened her eyes, turning over to grab for the phone. She dialed her cameraman. 'Jack, meet me downstairs immediately with Nick. Is the equipment in the car?'

The men inside the Land Rovers looked fit enough to hold off a Marine battalion. Most of them were equipped with M-16 or semi-automatic A R-15 rifles. One had a Uzi sub-machine-gun slung over his shoulder and another carried a grenade launcher. They all had plenty of spare ammunition.

El Jefe sat in the driver's seat. The bald stocky man pulled over his pump-action twelve-gauge shotgun to give Martin space on the passenger seat beside him. An automatic pistol was strapped to his belt. He just asked, '*Adonde?*'

Martin explained without wasting any time. *El Jefe* started the engine, lumbering out of the parking lot. The second Land Rover followed closely behind.

Jane just managed to catch sight of Martin closing the door of the Land Rover as she peeked around the corner of the entrance to the hotel. Both Land Rovers were turning into the street when Jack Haines and the soundman caught up with her.

Traffic was light going out of Santo Domingo and they managed to keep the two Land Rovers in sight all along the coastal highway. At the turnoff on to the road up into the mountains they almost lost them. But Jack Haines, who was driving, had once worked as a licensed PI. He turned the right way almost by instinct. Both Land Rovers became visible again as the road flattened out, only distinguishable in the dark by their lights.

But now that they were on the twists and turns nearing the final stretch before the dirt road to the plantation, Jack Haines had to admit that his instincts were failing him. They had lost the Land Rovers completely and the thickening vegetation made any prospect of catching sight of them remote. 'I don't think we stand a chance, Jane,' he said.

'Just a bit further, Jack.'

He drove on. The night was very black, with practically no moon. At one point he nearly drove off the road. Jack was getting disoriented and dizzy. 'It's no use, Jane, if we go on we may not make it back down to the coast.'

Jane had to find out what Martin was up to. The thought that he could end up getting the better of her infuriated her professional pride. The smile which had stayed with her since the hotel left her face. At that moment, a caravan of three cars overtook them very fast.

'Follow them, Jack, maybe they are going to the same place.'

Martin's drive with *El Jefe* had been mostly silent, limited to directions and occasional small talk. *El Jefe* finally offered one of his Marlboros, observing '*Estas*

147

nervioso' as if Martin had no reason to be. He accepted the cigarette gladly, having forgotten his back in his hotel room. Martin could not help the feeling that events were getting out of control. He no longer had any certainty of how this whole mess would turn out.

So Lopwitz had thought that operating in a guerrilla environment would be about as smooth as any back-handed business maneuver on Wall Street; that pulling off a terrorist kidnapping would be nothing more than an exotic twist to an otherwise straightforward corporate transaction. Men like Lopwitz ignored a lot of things, Martin thought as he exhaled the tobacco smoke and looked out of his window into the darkness. The price of failure in an operation such as this one was not reflected in changing green numbers on a computer screen but in stinking cold flesh lying in puddles of blood with pierced intestines.

For all he knew, the ELD could have taken the house by now, slaughtering everyone and taking Clark hostage for real, since they knew that a nice tidy ransom was being negotiated for him. And Nora, God knows what they would do to Nora. But Carlos would have certainly called again if there had been any indication of an attack on the house, he reassured himself – but not if the telephone lines had been cut, that possibility suddenly loomed before him, maybe it would have been wiser to evacuate.

As they turned into the dirt road for the final approach to the plantation, *El Jefe* started to talk about how much he looked forward to shooting it out with the ELD. 'All of my men are former police and soldiers. The best always leave the armed forces early and go to work for private companies like mine. We earn more money and even have better weapons. You know, when I was sergeant in our army, I trained for three months with your country's special forces in Fort Bragg. If we were turned loose on the Communists in this country, there would not be one of them left.'

Martin allowed himself to reflect for a moment on the unique alliance he had patched together; a right-wing mercenary death squad protecting a budding revolutionary leftist group holding an American businessman hostage. He thought it best not to risk *El Jefe*'s group getting too close to FART or John Clark. 'I think that in order not to cause any unnecessary alarm or discomfort to the people inside the house, it might be best for you to deploy your men around the grounds, *Jefe*'.

He readily agreed. It was the way that he would normally proceed in such circumstances, the man assured Martin. The Land Rover kept rumbling at high speed over the worsening road, taking a sharp turn on to the final stretch.

When they got to the clearing in front of the house, Martin was relieved to see that all looked normal. He noticed no one outside the house, which was probably a sensible precaution, and the car was still parked outside. He breathed a sigh of relief and told *El Jefe* to toot the horn four times, the agreed signal.

Carlos quickly emerged on to the front porch. Martin got out of the Land Rover, running across the grounds and bounding up the front steps to Carlos who greeted him like a long lost brother, tears and all.

El Jefe went to work dividing up his men. Five of them with the grenade rifle would take up positions near the road to cover the main approach. Two, including the man with the Uzi, would guard the rear entrance to the house. Two others would take up positions at the front while the remaining two would stay with him in the Land Rover, disposed to cover any blindspots or reinforce the other positions. He would communicate with his various positions by walkie-talkie.

Jane Winter and her crew had followed the second caravan of cars down the worsening dirt road and thickening foliage, keeping a safe distance. Suddenly, she noticed the headlights about a hundred yards in front of her going off. She immediately told Jack Haines to follow suit. They were engulfed in darkness when shots rang out. Then, the road in front of them was lit up by the orange flash of an explosion. The sound reverberated as the crackling of automatic rifle fire intensified and flames ripped all through the leading car of the three they had followed. It had obviously been hit by either a bazooka or grenade. A full battle was now in progress.

'I think we should get the fuck out of here.'

'Hell, no, Jack, with our infra-red equipment we can get some great pictures. Just get the car off the road.' She strained her eyes. 'I think I see an elevation there to the right.' Jane pointed through the car window towards the forest. 'From there we should be able to do some good filming.'

Jack knew better than to argue with Jane when she thought she was on to a good story. He managed to get the Mercedes to the foot of a mound, which they went on to climb. They got behind a tall clump of grass and started filming. The camera with the infra-red filter began to roll just in time to catch two of the ambushed men taking one of their wounded to safety behind the rear car. The flames from the burning vehicle actually provided plenty of natural light. Then another rocket grenade crashed nearby, missing the other two vehicles. The exchange of automatic rifle fire became louder as three more men arrived to take cover behind the rear car. Through the camera, Jack was able to see one of them huddle briefly with the two who were already there. The others kept shooting with what looked like AK–47s. As the brief huddle broke up, the two men who had been there first let off a series of rounds on full automatic while the other three ran into the undergrowth on their left for what looked like a flanking maneuver.

Carlos had given Martin the ·45 automatic. He was packing bullets into the magazine when he heard the first grenade go off. He had not arrived with the protection a moment too soon. How many were there? He kept inserting the bullets one at a time, hoping to get in the full load of ten. But the coil inside the clip was very tight, and the gun might jam if he had to use it. He stopped with nine and eased the loaded clip into the pistol butt, cocked it and pressed the safety-catch.

Martin had learned to shoot at the private range of a former FBI weapons instructor in Northern Virginia. He went out there to practice on most weekends, learning early on, much to his astonishment, that he was a natural shot.

As the sounds of battle grew outside, Martin checked around the house to make sure that everyone manned his station. *Tres* with his shotgun was barricaded behind a pile of furniture blocking the stairway to the second floor. He had a clear range of fire over the front entrance. Luis and *Cinco* were on the second floor outside Clark's room with a ·38 revolver between them, more for the purpose of making sure Clark stayed in than with the hope of keeping anyone out, if it came to that. Carlos and *Dos*, with one revolver each, covered the back of the living-room which gave on to the garden with the pool. It was being guarded from the outside by two of *El Jefe*'s men with the Uzi and an M-16. All the shutters and curtains were drawn.

Martin now heard the sound of the second grenade exploding. *El Jefe* was shouting out orders for his men to reinforce the roadside. Two had been hit, Martin heard him yell.

As Martin took his place behind an upturned couch at the front end of the living-room, covering the side of the entrance, he heard heavy automatic fire coming near the house. In the next few seconds it came very close. Rounds started piercing windows, shattering glass and ripping through curtains.

The explosive spray of sub-machine-gun fire was now also audible from around the back. Carlos and *Dos* hit the floor as a line of rounds sliced through the back entrance. Uninterrupted shooting followed in a continuous duel between the guards outside and the attackers.

Suddenly, there was a full automatic discharge of assault rifles right on the front porch. One of the living-room windows disintegrated. The wood shutter splintered and the curtain came down as one of *El Jefe*'s men tumbled through it, falling inside with his chest ripped open. Martin thought of trying to make for the M–16 which lay next to the mangled body. But at that instant heavy rounds from an AK–47 stitched the front door from close range. Splinters of wood and metal now filled the entrance hall as the front lock was shot through. The door swung open and a camouflaged figure rushed in spraying fire from his automatic rifle.

Tres's double shotgun blast from the top of the stairs seemed to unsteady the attacker sufficiently for Martin to take aim with the ·45 and squeeze off five rounds. The attacker crouched but not in time and his body collapsed in the entrance hall. That instant another figure appeared, laying heavy automatic fire into the living-room and the stairway, within inches of Martin, ripping through the upholstery and metal springs of the couch. As he prepared for certain death, Martin heard strong blasts from outside. When he looked up from the floor, the second attacker was lying on his face in the entrance way, his back a splattered blood-soaked mess.

The sound of sub-machine-gun bursts was still distinct outside, but growing fainter as Martin began picking himself up, amazed that he was alive. Feathers from the bullet-riddled cushions were still flying. Then *El Jefe* hurried into the entrance way, holding up his pump-action shotgun. He kicked over the two dead bodies in front of him. '*Estan todos bien?*' he shouted. Martin walked over to him still clutching his ·45 and put his arm around the old man in silent thanks.

He looked out of the destroyed entrance to see short bursts of white/yellow light coming from the sub-machine-gun of a third attacker who was covering his escape into the surrounding bush. He also saw the body of another of *El Jefe*'s men lying on the ground in front moaning from what appeared to be a leg wound. Another was kneeling nearby firing at the man escaping into the tall grass and trees.

'We have to find and neutralize him,' said *El Jefe*. 'He could start sniping at my men holding the intersection. We've taken serious casualties. This attack group is super-trained.' He gestured at the kneeling rifleman who was now fitting another clip into his M-16. 'He is the only one I can spare.'

Martin could read his thoughts. 'I will go with him.'

El Jefe unholstered his 9mm Browning automatic, handing it to Martin. 'It's fully loaded.'

Martin took the pistol and rushed towards the undergrowth. The man with the M-16 followed closely behind. At that moment there was another explosion near the intersection.

Jane Winter and her crew managed to film the exact moment when the rocket grenade tore through the engine of the second car, orange flames and sparks shooting into the air. As the gasoline caught fire and the car burst into flames, it lit up two men running towards the last able vehicle, carrying a wounded man between them while a third provided covering fire. But a steady barrage of automatic rounds cut one of them down. The injured man was now abandoned as the lone survivor broke and ran for the car which already had the engine started. The one providing the cover fire now also ran for his life, just managing to jump into the car as it rumbled and screeched into a U-turn, hitting a tree as it skidded on some mud and then tore up the dirt road. It brushed the spot from where the television crew were filming.

The shooting had stopped. The only sounds now came from the exploding car. Jack Haines put down his camera. 'We better get the hell outa here.' They quietly made their way down through the thick under-growth. As they arrived at their Mercedes, a bloodied figure emerged limping from the opposite side of the road, holding a sub-machine-gun to them. Jane screamed.

The bottom of his leg dripped blood from what was obviously a bullet injury. He shook all over as his blackened face contorted in panic. He grabbed Jane by the hair, arm-locking her throat as he squeezed the barrel of his sub-machine-gun to her temple. He wanted them to drive him into Santo Domingo. As he bolted his sub-machine-gun and gestured towards the car, two shots rang out. Blood splattered all over Jane's face as his machine gun dropped, his arm eased off her throat and he crumpled to the ground.

She turned to see Martin, both of his hands firmly gripped around a smoking automatic pistol. He had just put two shots straight through her assailant's head. Another man carrying an M-16 rustled out of the bushes behind him.

She fell in love.

Teresa had been in bed with *Comandante Nueve*, who had demanded her favors that night, when they got the news at five in the morning. They were now back in his office along with *Comandante Cuatro* and a ban-daged survivor of the decimated raiding party, whose leader, *Comandante Siete*, had not made it back. *Nueve* was raging.

'*Es imposible!* It's a trick! I'm telling you it's a filthy trick!' He pounded his desk.

But Teresa was no longer listening. *Comandante Siete*, whom she knew as Manolo, had been her secret lover for many years. He had hardly had a moment to spend alone with her since getting back from Nicaragua. Now, he was presumed dead. She could not control her tears.

'I want to call a full meeting of the executive committee for this afternoon,' he kept shouting at *Cuatro*. 'Do you understand? A full meeting this very afternoon! This is not going to go unanswered! We will respond!'

But Teresa no longer felt like she was part of *Nueve*'s world. She had hated sucking off his fat penis that night, which is all that he ever wanted her for, wishing the whole time that it could be Manolo. And now . . . now. Tears flowed.

'You get word to all my other seven *comandantes* that I want them here for a meeting this afternoon!' *Nueve* pounded his desk again as *Cuatro* took the order. Teresa could only think of running, running far away. But where would she run to? Brian.

She would run to Brian Thorpe.

Martin awoke, suddenly, in the Land Rover, his mind racing over the terrifying events of the night. But the slamming of the driver's door and the sight of white-coated medics gathering outside to take down the three wounded men lying in the rear of the Land Rover filled him with the reality of what had transpired: pitched combat, coming within a hair's breadth of getting killed himself, killing a man for the first time in his life and saving the life of a beautiful woman, a TV star at that, to whom he had made love only hours before.

They were now parked in front of the emergency ward of the General Hospital of Santo Domingo, a dilapidated structure built thirty years ago. He turned to look back. One man was being helped out. He limped on one leg while holding up the other which was wrapped in a blood-soaked bandage. Both his arms were around the shoulders of two nurses who slowly walked him into the open entrance.

The other two men, too badly wounded to move, were being placed on stretchers. A white-coated doctor crouched his way into the back of the Land Rover, examining them with his stethoscope. The sweet smell of blood was all-pervasive. The doctor ordered both men to be rushed to surgery.

Vivid images of the rest of the battle's aftermath cascaded through Martin's mind. Still in shock, Jane Winter had flung herself into his arms. He had used his shirt to wipe the blood off her face. After some initial sobbing she started to kiss him and thank him for saving her life.

He didn't even bother to ask what they were doing there. She had obviously followed him. 'You're out of your goddam mind, Jane, are you crazy or something?' He pointed at the film camera Jack Haines was still carrying. 'I'm keeping that film. Will you kindly hand it to me?'

They were in no position to argue. Jane just nodded. Jack opened up the camera and tossed the cassette to Martin.

'Was this what that telephone conversation in your room was all about?' Jane worked up the gumption to ask as Martin saw them into their Mercedes.

He didn't answer, just saying, 'I'll see you back at the hotel. I trust you won't say a word to anyone.'

When Martin got back to the house, *El Jefe* was bringing his wounded inside. *Dos* and *Cinco* were tearing bedsheets into bandages as Carlos applied a tourniquet to the one with the leg wound. *Tres* had miraculously emerged unscathed from under the pile of furniture which had protected him from countless

AK-47 and sub-machine-gun rounds and was hustling John Clark III up the stairs, together with Luis. Nora stood around, her body overflowing from a towel, gazing in disbelief at the battle-scarred living-room.

When Carlos saw Martin, he left *Dos* with the tourniquet, rushing up to take him aside and explain that Clark had run down the stairs after the shooting, screaming about what was going on and demanding an explanation. The battle had clearly brought him out of the erotic stupor into which Nora had so artfully seduced him. Martin told Carlos to get up there and tranquilize him again, and sent Nora up after him to help calm Clark down.

El Jefe had been too busy caring for his wounded to pay much attention to Clark or Nora. Satisfied with the well-above market price of sixty thousand dollars which Martin had agreed to pay for his services, he hadn't raised any troublesome questions until then. But when the stocky man took a minute to tell Martin that he had lost two men and needed to rush his three seriously wounded to hospital, he inquired who the other American was. Martin just told him that it was some rich American having a secret holiday here with his mistress. *El Jefe* appeared to accept the explanation. Martin just hoped he hadn't had a close enough look to recognize Clark from the newspapers. What if he had? Martin had no plans to deal with such an eventuality, except possibly to offer more money. What if he told someone in the police force who was not in on the kidnapping? Colonel Ventura and maybe Major Otero were covering up, but how many other subordinates could be trusted?

As Martin struggled with these questions Carlos found a moment, between Clark's forceful sedation and the bandaging of a bullet-pierced ribcage, to tell him that the whole charade could not last any longer. Martin hardly needed to be told.

Barely confident that Carlos and the rest of FART

could hold things together for a little while longer, and hardly trusting the six men whom *El Jefe* was leaving behind to guard the safe house, Martin decided to hitch a ride back to Santo Domingo with the wounded.

As they were starting up the Land Rover, the two men *El Jefe* had sent out to comb the area around the intersection, where the main fighting had taken place, came back carrying another injured man. It was one of the ELD attack force who had been forgotten or left behind with shoulder and leg wounds from shrapnel. He said his name was Manolo.

El Jefe ordered him shot. A similar fate awaited the other ELD prisoner in the basement.

Should he just settle immediaely for whatever the ransom negotiators offered and call Lopwitz with a *fait accompli*? What would Lopwitz's reaction be when he found out about what had happened? Could he trust Jane Winter to keep her mouth shut? Could he perhaps use her to extricate himself from this increasingly messy affair. As Martin kept turning over these questions in his fatigued state, *El Jefe* got back into the car, slammed his door shut and said, 'Now I take you to hotel.'

Brian Thorpe was doing his press-ups when the telephone rang. Teresa was calling from downstairs. Could she come up? She sounded sullen. Thorpe told her that he would leave the door open, called room service for coffee and went into the bathroom to shower and shave.

When he came out again, in his kimono with a towel hanging around his neck, Teresa was sitting by the window. Her face was puffy from crying. As she turned to look at him, tears streamed down her cheeks. She spoke between sobs. 'Brian, the ELD tried to raid the safe house where FART is holding Clark.'

'What!' Thorpe bounded over to Teresa, shaking her by the shoulders. 'What!'

'Oh, please, Brian, don't hurt me. I had no idea of it until just over an hour ago. I'm suffering enough . . . a very . . . a very good close friend of mine who led the assault got killed . . . It was a massacre.'

He still held her by the shoulder. 'What did the bloody ELD have in mind?'

'They . . . they wanted to kill off the FART and . . . and take the hostage themselves.'

Thorpe let go of her, passing a hand through his wet hair, his eyes popping out as he realized the terrifying implications. The FART could even think that he had something to do with it. 'They failed in this attempt, presumably?'

Teresa nodded, still sobbing. 'Nobody understands it. It was like an army camp out there. The ELD sent twelve of its best men just back from guerrilla training in Nicaragua . . . less than half made it back alive. Two of their cars were destroyed by rocket grenades.'

Thorpe wanted to ask Teresa where the safe house was located. But she was crying too much. Besides, that was of academic interest at this point. The only thing that mattered now was getting John Clark out of there as soon as possible – if he was still alive – paying his full coverage if necessary. He had overplayed his hand. Thorpe felt like an idiot. He picked up the phone to dial Tom's room. They had to communicate with FART immediately.

Martin staggered up the front steps to the hotel entrance. He had now gone two nights without proper sleep and felt spent. He stiffened up as best he could when he asked for his keys at reception. He looked as if he had been through . . . what he had just been through. His shirt was caked with dried blood. The concierge could not help a certain inquiring glance. Martin felt obliged to explain that he had been in a car accident, expressing thanks for some concerned comment as he was handed the keys, accompanied by a message. Lopwitz had called, leaving a number where he could be reached in Panama. The prospect of speaking with Lopwitz now was enough to loosen his bowels which he had kept tightly contracted since his awakening outside the hospital. It would not wait until he got to his room.

He walked across the lobby to the men's lavatory, automatically going into the right-hand booth which had been serving as the drop in his communications with the ransom negotiators. After he was finished Martin decided to take a look, since he was there anyway. He lifted the cover off the cistern, and fished out an envelope sealed in plastic.

All it took was a glance at the first sentence to inject his drained body with a flash of energy: 'We double our ransom offer to twenty million dollars US pending your release of Jonathan Clark, alive, in the next twenty-four hours . . .'

'. . . Well done, Martin, I knew you could do it . . .' Lopwitz was speaking from the terrace of his eleventh-floor suite at the Mariot Hotel in Panama City. His view overlooked a spacious tropical garden at the back of the hotel, one of the few pretty sites in an otherwise drab and dreary town. A breakfast tray was laid out on a low table in front of him. Over the distant haze, it was just possible to make out the masts of a ship moving up into one of the locks through the canal. '. . . But try to get it just a bit higher. Say that we will settle at twenty-two and a half. That's still two million within his coverage . . . after that little

160

gunslinging you had last night it's going to be necessary to make a few more payoffs down there. I want
twenty-one million to be wired into an account I'm
setting up over here and one and half million to be
handed in cash over there for your share, FART's and
our expenses . . .'

When he put down the phone, Lopwitz drained his
coffee cup and lit a pipeful of Jamaican Rum tobacco.
He sat back to enjoy the view with the slightly dizzy-
ing sensation of an early-morning smoke. Before talking with Martin he had spoken with Ventura, who
already knew everything about the previous night's
battle at the Plantacion de Arguelles. The police chief
was highly upset, saying that by contracting the bodyguard service through Major Otero, Martin had
directly implicated the police force in the kidnapping.
'This was not our original deal, Mr Weinstein.' Lopwitz had to admit that Ventura had a point. The price
the Colonel now demanded was an extra million
dollars and the extermination of the entire FART
once John Clark had been released. He could hold it
up as an anti-terrorist victory before his superiors to
get a promotion.

Lopwitz might have spared Martin, making sure that
he got out of Santo Domingo before the death squad
which was now guarding the safe house turned its guns
on Carlos and his group, paying him his half-million
dollar share from the ransom money in Panama. But
what he had just heard made that impossible. The boy
was an incurable romantic. His brains were stuck
between his legs and there was nothing anyone could
do to pull them out. Saving the life of that intruding
television news starlet who followed him out there,
Lopwitz thought, he might just as well have let the
ELD resolve that problem for him as well.

He had better hedge his bets, Lopwitz started to
realize. Maybe a quiet chat with Dick Stewart in Washington would be in order at this stage.

12

The American wearing sunglasses and a sports shirt moved through Santo Domingo's open market. It was always crowded, especially on a Saturday. The fish stalls were still receiving the night's fresh catch while women in long colourful skirts bargained with the vendors. Many balanced baskets on their heads, piled high with fruits and vegetables. Some breastfed babies while going about their chores. The loud, shrill voices of lottery ticket salesmen announced that week's numbers. Groups of men in their guayaberas savoring hand-rolled cigars discussed results from the previous week's draw with the seriousness of tradesmen on the stock exchange floor.

It was near the lottery stand where the American stopped at a small open bar, ordering *un cortado*, or small coffee with a little milk. He sipped it and looked around, removing his sunglasses, twice. A dark man in an unbuttoned shirt then moved next to him, ordering the same then commenting, 'They say that *El Gordo* for this week will have a five and a two in it.'

'I've been told that it will be a seven and a three.' Steven Drysdale had received a telephone call from the dark man's wife that morning simply giving him the numbers fifty-two and seventy-three. In that combination the four digits meant that he should go for a drop at the usual place. It was Drysdale's backup system of communicating with his source inside the ELD when there was urgent information to pass on and not the necessary time or safety to arrange a direct meeting. They could only have regular interviews twice a month. For cases like today's the dark-skinned lottery speculator was their cutout.

Having reassured each other that they were not being followed or observed, the dark man slipped five lottery tickets into an envelope, handing it to Drysdale, who produced the amount of cash which would normally correspond to such a purchase. After counting his money, the seller sipped down the last drop of his coffee and melted into the crowd. Drysdale lingered on a few minutes, drinking a second *cortado*, and then disappeared into the nearest side-street.

Sitting at the desk of his apartment with the window curtains securely drawn, Drysdale emptied the five lottery tickets from the envelope and pulled out a blank sheet of paper which was folded inside of it. He then soaked a piece of cloth in cologne and gently passed it over the blank sheet. The words of the message written in invisible ink now stood out.

It told him of the attempt by the ELD to raid the safe house where John Clark was being held. The location, time and circumstances of the armed encounter corroborated information which he had already received that morning. Knowing the reason behind the incident, Drysdale was now one hundred percent certain of who could get him to FART.

'. . . As soon as Clark is awake and fed and feeling like himself again, put him on the phone to room 310 at the Hotel Lima. They have a tape recording of his voice which they will compare with the voice on the phone in order to check his identity. They will also ask him a series of personal questions about his childhood. He needs to be able to answer them accurately, so he has to be alert, Carlos . . .' Martin was speaking from a public telephone booth inside a restaurant in the center of Santo Domingo. He could no longer be sure that he was not being observed or listened to in his hotel.

Less than an hour ago he had received the final reply from the ransom negotiators, agreeing to twenty-two and a half million dollars and stipulating conditions for the handover. Twenty-one million would be wired to the offshore account in Panama while one and a half million would be delivered in cash to Santo Domingo as soon as they had the necessary proof that John Clark was alive. They would leave it up to FART to decide where the cash should be deposited. The movement of the money would take twenty-four hours and they expected Clark to be released no later than twelve hours after the ransom had been paid.

Martin emerged from the booth and went back to his table to pick up the tab. He had eaten the traditional local lunch of roast pork, rice and black beans with fried bananas for dessert. That he could get some sleep now was the only thing he could think of as he went out into the busy downtown street for a taxi. He now had someone permanently on his tail.

There was consternation among the assembled. *Comandante Nueve*'s most faithful follower, *Comandante Uno*, cheered him on: '*Eso es! A sus ordenes mi lider maximo!*' But others were not so sure.

Comandante Ocho cautioned, 'Plan Zero? But we are not yet prepared.' He exhaled a stream of smoke from his cigar. 'The arms from Cuba have not arrived.'

Only half of *Nueve*'s eight other *comandantes* had been able to make the hastily convened war council. One was presumed dead from last night, two were too far in the interior of the country to be able to get to Santo Domingo, and another could not move for security reasons.

'We have the necessary arms to mount the initial attacks, to show the world who are the real leaders of the revolution in the Republica Dominicana and demonstrate that it has really begun.' For *Nueve* there was no turning back. 'Maybe that is what Fidel Castro needs to hurry up his ass. He has been promising to send us the arms now for six months.'

'But Fidel said to wait,' *Ocho* insisted, wiping sweat off his brow.

'I don't care what Fidel said.' *Comandante Nueve* leaned over his desk. 'He is too busy driving Gina Lollobrigida around in his jeep!' He clenched his fists. 'In the meantime we are ridiculed, upstaged and tricked by clowns like FART and by whoever the devil is behind them! No, *companeros*, we can wait no longer. We lost seven of our best men last night and we must demonstrate the terrible revenge of which we are capable. We will act now and then others will act for us.'

Before the meeting, *Comandante Nueve* had received a call from his contact in Miami which had alarmed him even more. The Arguelles house had been rented nearly two months ago to an American by the name of Douglas Weinstein, probably an assumed name. He would do some further checking, the man in Miami had told *Nueve*.

Martin had been awakened in the middle of the afternoon by Carlos, who simply said three words, 'All is well.' It meant that the ransom negotiators had been satisfied in their telephone interview with John Clark. The only thing left to be done was to communicate to the negotiators specific instructions on where and how to deliver the ransom. Any moment there would be a call from Lopwitz with the number of the account in Panama.

Despite his groggy state, Martin could not sleep any more. He sat on his bed smoking, getting more nervous by the minute. No longer certain that his communications were secure, he was considering changing the drop for his ransom notes. If anyone intercepted the next message uncovering the location for the pickup in Santo Domingo, and the account in Panama, that would be the end.

Lopwitz was re-entering his suite at the Panama City Mariot, highly satisfied with the lunch and subsequent two-hour meeting with his Panamanian banker and an excellent local attorney, *Señor* Miranda. He had the new account number to give Martin, opened through a corporate identity which was being registered by the lawyer. But that was not the account that would actually receive the money. Local banking practices made it possible to arrange anything in Panama, at a price. The moment the standby telex notice was received for the impending transfer of twenty-one million dollars to the account number which he was going to give Martin, Miranda, acting on behalf of the dummy corporation, would erase that account, diverting the transfer into another number that he would activate in the name of the company. Within twenty-four hours of that operation, the company would be liquidated and the money divided and passed through ten other accounts that would be opened up in the names of different companies in Panama, the Cayman Islands, the Bahamas, Luxembourg, Lichtenstein, Gibraltar, Bahrain and Hong Kong. There, the money would sit, gaining interest until Lopwitz, working through third parties, of course, opened up the offshore bank that would extend the bail-out loan to the Sanitex Equipment Corporation in return for majority ownership. His

Panamanian lawyer would cut a hefty slice from the profits of the subsequent liquidation of Sanitex, as would the banker who would, in effect, hold a large portion of the stock. Lopwitz figured that he would end up with seventy-five percent for himself. He picked up the phone to call Martin, to give him the number of his new account.

The taxi pulled up at the seafront drive or 'malecón', just where it intersected with the Avenida de la Independencia. It was a short ride from the hotel, as are most places in Santo Domingo. Tom Cross emerged from the back seat, told the driver to wait, as he had been instructed to do, and walked up to a litter basket by the side of the nearest bench behind the sea wall. He searched a bit among the trash before finding the envelope marked by three crosses. The note inside it told him to walk to the next litter basket about thirty yards away.

It was early evening and the palm-shaded malecón was filling up with strollers, many of them young lovers walking arm in arm, exchanging kisses and lovebites with the usual Latin propensity for public displays of affection. Across the road, Martin sat at a table in an open café, observing Cross. He had rung the negotiators from there, barely a quarter of an hour ago, telling them the location of the note which Cross had just picked up. It was a way of making sure that if he was being followed, at least no one would be able to intercept the all-important message without his knowledge. From where he sat, which was on an elevated position, Martin had a clear line of vision to both litter baskets.

What was occurring on the bench next to the second litter basket, however, began disturbing Martin, as well as Tom Cross who was approaching it. A teenage couple were sitting on it and necking passionately. As Cross reached the litter basket the boy was practically on top of the girl, his hand feeling its way up to the plump breast beneath her T-shirt. Cross thought of waiting nearby until the moment of passion had spent itself.

But heaven knew how long that would take and if FART were watching him, as would almost certainly be the case, it could send the wrong signal. For all he knew, the randy couple could be shadowing him. He started rummaging through the litter. The girl's protestations grew louder as the boy tried to lift her skirt. Just as he found the envelope with the three crosses, the action on the bench froze. The large mulatto boy looked up at Cross as the girl pulled her skirt back down. They started hurling insults at him as he apologetically backed off with the two envelopes towards his waiting taxi.

Back in his hotel room, Martin slipped into a fresh shirt. He had just had a long hot shower and felt better. Jane Winter was meeting him for dinner at nine. As he knotted his tie in the mirror, there was a knock at the door. Thinking that it could be Jane getting impatient again, he went to open it, but hesitated as his hand touched the knob. 'Who is it?' Martin even thought of reaching for the ·45 automatic which Carlos had let him keep. It dawned on him that anything could happen in any moment.

'I'm Steven Drysdale from the American Embassy, we met in the bar a few nights ago. I would like to have a word with you.'

Martin's heart skipped a beat. 'I'm getting ready to go out, Mr Drysdale. May I ask what this is about?'

'I think we'd better talk inside, Mr Martin.'

The door swung open and Drysdale strolled in

whistling, just slightly. He nodded a silent greeting at Martin before going to sit on one of the armchairs near the window. Martin sat on the hard-backed desk chair facing him. 'What can I do for you, Mr Drysdale?'

'It should be a question of what we can do for you, Mr Martin. If you don't realize the kind of danger you are in, you must be more of a fool than I think you are. And if you think that you are going to get out of Santo Domingo alive without our help you had better think twice.'

A feeling of *déjà vu* crept into Martin, but he just said, 'I don't think I understand what you mean.'

'Don't play games with me, pal.' Steve Drysdale leaned over as he threw off his seersucker jacket to reveal a shoulder holster strapped over his sports shirt with what Martin recognized to be a ·22 Beretta tucked inside. 'I know all about your background. Computers, my ass, you have worked as a terrorism analyst with Security International in Virginia for more than five years. Previous to that you were an investigative reporter for a London newspaper, uncovering spy intrigues and military coups in Portugal and Spain. Now you are here running your own terrorist operation and we want to find out a little bit about it.'

'Are you CIA?'

'What do you think, Martin? We've been shadowing your movements and today we realize that we aren't the only ones. Which is what decided me on coming to see you now because there is no way that we are going to get too many questions answered when we find your body in an open grave.'

Martin could fake it no longer. 'Who wants to kill me?' was the only thing he could think of to say.

'You were responsible for the deaths of over a half-dozen of the ELD's best men last night. How many more fucking enemies do you need?'

Jane Winter couldn't be the one who had given him away, Martin was trying to comfort himself. She would have no way of knowing that it was the ELD who were assaulting the house or the amount of casualties. He was confirmed in his belief by what Drysdale went on to say.

'Now, we want to know what your role is exactly in this Clark kidnapping and with FART. Why are you protecting them, in other words? What are you up to?'

El Jefe, it must have been *El Jefe* who told them, thought Martin. He is the only one who got a look at Clark. He is probably on the CIA payroll ... Should have known. But what else could he have done? There was only one way to cover himself. If the beans were going to spill, he didn't want to be the one holding the bag. 'Why don't you ask the police? They are in this as deep as I am.'

'We know they are. Those guys you hired to shoot it out with ELD at the FART safe house last night practically are the police. But we don't want them to know that we know, Martin. Not just yet, anyway, because they may decide to do something rash if it gets embarrassing, like kill you all off.'

Drysdale let his words sink in as Martin fished around for a cigarette. When it was lit, the CIA operative continued, more relaxed now, 'No, Martin, we aren't interested in getting information from the police. We aren't even interested in whatever ransom it is you are negotiating. What we are interested in is talking with the leader of FART. Is that you?'

13

Martin emerged from the front entrance of the Hotel Lima with Jane Winter on his arm. She was all smiles, her body lithe and bouncy in an elegant sleeveless dress. The electricity between them was enough to send sparks flying. But for Martin, the double jeopardy in which he was now caught hung like a rain cloud over the shining moment.

Once in the back seat of the chauffeured Mercedes, Jane snuggled close to him. They drove down the *avenida* and turned on to the *malecón*.

The still sea beyond the palm trees mirrored a reflection of a new moon. On the inland side, an unbroken row of restaurants and cafés was filled to capacity. Political strife, terrorism, guerrilla war and martial law seemed to have less effect on the leisurely life of Dominicans than the passing thunder-showers.

It was a beautiful evening and Martin figured that he'd better enjoy it because it could be his last. His life had become entirely compromised. It no longer belonged to him. He could be sold out, killed, eliminated, destroyed and used at the mere whim or convenience of individuals with conflicting interests and any recourse to escape the situation promised a fate of equal danger.

Martin had not given Drysdale any names – a card which he would hope to play with Lopwitz if it became necessary. But he had told him pretty much everything else. His executive role in a terrorist kidnapping and massive insurance fraud was now known to the US government, and – he looked at Jane next to him – only a breath away from becoming public knowledge as well. Whatever guarantees of safety and confidentiality the CIA offered him now were, ultimately, empty. If events over which he had no control moved in certain directions, he would be sacrificed, of that Martin was certain.

There was one other thing that Martin had not told Drysdale, the time or location for tomorrow's pick-up of the one and a half million dollars. It was another card that he would keep close to his chest. He was supposed to meet Drysdale at an address he had been given, tomorrow morning at nine.

Jane interrupted his thoughts. 'You are being awfully quiet.' The seafront was now behind them. The car wound its way past rows of old stone houses on its climb into the historic colonial part of Santo Domingo.

'Combat fatigue, maybe,' he said lightly.

'Not too much, I hope,' she whispered as she wrapped her arms around him. Martin's lips met hers.

The car now slowly angled its way into the narrowest cobbled arteries of the historical section. The illuminated entrance of the restaurant where they were going appeared, with the parapeted walls of the sixteenth-century Spanish fortress silhouetted beyond.

'Martin, can't you just tell me what was in that place last night that was worth the Normandy invasion? I realize I'm a journalist, but please trust me. It won't go beyond us.'

How many other people will it not go beyond, Martin wondered as the car pulled in front of the two eighteenth-century ship-lamps that flanked the restaurant's doorway. He just said, 'We're here.'

He got out of the car first, taking Jane's hand as she stepped out and they entered the candlelit interior with its polished old wood furniture and bare stone walls. The head waiter instantly attended them and they were shown to the table on the terrace which Martin had reserved in Jane's name.

The moonlit bay opened before them, ships lay peacefully at anchor in the natural harbor and dispersed rows of lights shone from the fishermen's shacks across the water. Small boats bobbed near their moorings. Immediately below their terrace a narrow walkway wound down to the water's edge and the sound of merengue music was just audible from the open doorway of a seaside bar.

White-jacketed waiters with polished brass buttons tended them, bringing warm bread, butter and plates of olives and chorizo. When they were given their menus, Jane ordered champagne.

They toasted. After taking their first sips, Jane turned to look at the view again. 'God, it's beautiful. It's so perfectly romantic.' She looked back at Martin. 'It's hard to believe that a man with your taste and sensitivity kills people for a sideline. Even if you did save my life.' She took his hand.

'That was a stupid thing you did last night, Jane.' Then he muttered, 'And don't try any clever angles to get information out of me.'

The waiter came back to take their order. They would have a cold soup to start with and then the speciality of the house, baked fish in clam sauce served with boiled potatoes.

'Martin, you've got to tell me what it is you are doing here. Forget for a moment that I'm a journalist and just see me as a woman who cares about you.' Her eyes watered.

'Jane . . . I . . .' Martin was having trouble getting the words out. He was all knotted up inside. A part of him wanted to trust her and say it all. But his mind said no.

'Martin, are you in some kind of trouble? Are you running death squads or something?'

He wanted to tell her. God, how he wanted to tell her. 'Jane, do you know anyone at the US Embassy here called Steven Drysdale?'

'No. Why?'

'Just wondered. Look, have you spoken about last night to anyone?'

'No, Martin, I haven't. I've kept my word. The only ones who know are my camera crew and they wouldn't talk about it. They appreciate being alive as much as I do. That's why I wish that you would cut out this cloak-and-dagger business with me and tell me what kind of mess you're in.'

'Would you keep a secret even if it was worth a Pulitzer prize?'

'Even if it was worth a Pulitzer prize.' She half-closed her eyes. 'I'm in your debt. I'm . . .' She flashed her long eyelashes. 'I'm very taken by you. If you are in some kind of fix, I will try to help you. Just tell me. Please tell me.' She kept her hand in his, her eyes turning liquid.

Her touch and her look couldn't lie even if her words could. At that moment, the words of the merengue singing from the seaside bar below filled Martin's ears. He forgot about the dangers that surrounded him and could only think of loving her. It was as if Jane, the poetry, the soft melody and the warm salty breeze had filled him with a new certainty. The certainty of love and trust. The certainty of knowing that he could find it in another human being. A calmness set into his perturbed soul, as if he were inside the eye of the hurricane. He told her everything.

Jane listened intently without asking any questions. She understood. She had been compromised once. While covering a vice-presidential visit to Mexico some years ago, she had enjoyed a fling with an official of the Cuban Embassy who, as it turned out, was an operative of Castro's intelligence service, the

Direccion General de Inteligencia. He had fed her information about an assassination plot to kill the Vice President hatched by a group of Cuban exiles and Nicaraguan Contras. The story turned out to be a plant. Her meteoric career could have been ended there and then. But the CIA approached her, offering to cover up the worst aspects of the incident if she would do some work for them. She had traded favors with the Agency ever since.

The forested grounds surrounding the large suburban house were thick with fallen wet leaves. A freezing drizzle chilled the early morning. Lopwitz was having breakfast in Dick Stewart's double-glazed back porch.

Stewart, still in his pyjamas, bedroom slippers and woolen bathrobe, had gotten up to stoke the fire while Lopwitz sat, drinking down his fresh orange juice.

'Frankly, Herb, I think you have exceeded your limits this time.' He put down the poker and sank back into his feathery armchair.

'Come on, Dick, you can have full use of that off-shore bank I'm going to set up in Cayman. And when I've liquidated Sanitex Equipment, there will be a good slice of the action for you.'

'I still don't like it.'

'But, Dick, it doesn't involve you directly.'

'It involves us now.'

After Lopwitz had phoned him from Panama the previous day, Stewart had spoken to his friend who was head of the Latin American division and gotten directly in touch with the station chief in Santo Domingo. Mike Webb had given him all the information they had and told him that Drysdale was going to talk to Martin personally.

'Only inasmuch as . . .'

'Only inasmuch as you want us to cover up for you.' Stewart sipped his coffee.

'We've had this mutually beneficial relationship for years, Dick.'

'That may be so, Herb, but a kidnapping! What do you think the Agency is? A clearing house for criminal activities?'

Lopwitz said nothing. He just smiled.

'Well, not for your personal use, Herb.' Stewart passed a hand over his full head of white hair. He felt distinctly put upon.

'All that I'm asking you to do is to allow the episode to stand as is. As everyone believes it stands.' Lopwitz started to light his pipe. 'The whole thing is going to be over today. The ransom is being deposited in my Panama bank account this afternoon.'

'This is the last time, Herb. And the only thing that makes it possible to keep this under wraps is that one of our guys in Santo Domingo, this Steve Drysdale, is all gung ho about using this group which you set up . . . FART is it?'

Lopwitz nodded.

'Drysdale figures that since he is in a position to compromise the group, he can control FART to lever the revolutionary left in the Dominican Republic away from the hard-line Cuban-backed movement there, the ELD.'

'What do you mean?' Lopwitz leaned forward in his chair, puffing at his pipe a little frantically.

'With the publicity which this kidnapping of yours has generated, FART has gained a certain legitimacy in the eyes of pro-revolutionary forces. It's been the first group to hold an American hostage. So, it can now act as a competitive alternative to the ELD with covert American backing and direction. The ELD is afraid of this, Drysdale thinks, which is the reason why it tried to raid the safe house last night.'

'But . . .'

'In other words, by using FART, Drysdale figures that he can split and penetrate the far left, moving events down there in our direction. With their million-dollar share of the ransom, he calculates that he can finance the whole operation.'

'But . . .'

'Sounds like something of a harebrained scheme to me, but I reckon that's what these guys are paid to do. Must admit that there is a certain convenient logic in it.'

'But . . . there are certain problems.'

'Like what?'

'Because as soon as Clark gets released, Colonel Ventura is busting FART and blowing all of them away. It's part of my arrangement with him. He is supposed to be getting their share of the ransom.'

The morning heat began to evaporate the residue of that night's brief but heavy rainfall. Steam rose from the soaked pavement. The two tired sentries, inside their boxes on either side of the sheet metal gates to the police headquarters, waited impatiently. They had been at their posts most of the night and the guard should have been changed nearly a quarter of an hour ago.

As the sentry on the right removed his blue képi to wipe his brow with his sleeve, a car screeched to a stop in front of them. A pretty young girl hopped out, wearing a miniskirt, her braless breasts bouncing under a half-open shirt. She would just be a second, she said, had to go to pick something up.

She darted across the road and around the corner of the opposite block. The sentry moved towards her car with his M-1 rifle. 'Why does she park here when there is plenty of space across the road?' he wondered out loud. 'She must want something.' His last thought was a pleasant one. He would have barely had a fraction of a second to see and hear the full effect of five kilos of detonating C-4 plastic before he and the car disintegrated.

A broken torso was all that was left to see of the other sentry's corpse as mortar shells crashed into the interior of the police headquarters and a van rolled up to unload men in battledress who quickly moved through the blown-out gates and collapsed walls. Firing AK-47 assault rifles, they took cover behind rubble left by the explosion to avoid returning fire. A squeeze on the trigger of an RPG 7 rocket launcher was all it took to eliminate the resistance by a handful of policemen who were shooting from behind an overturned jeep. It burst into flames from a direct hit on the fuel tank, spreading more wreckage and hunks of dead flesh across the wasted grounds.

The ELD guerrillas now charged in past the burning jeep. One of them tripped over the body of a dead policeman and was hit by a rifle-round fired from inside the building. The others concentrated their automatic fire on the narrow window from where the shots had come. A second wave of attackers poured in to reinforce the initial assault force, taking positions to provide fierce covering fire as the nine men rushed across the rubble- and corpse-strewn courtyard. The gate into the interior building was blown open by another RPG round before they bounded up the steps and into the building with their AK-47s blazing, killing all that moved.

Martin was pushing hard into Jane. She had woken him up only moments before, placing a leg over his so that he could feel her growing moistness, inviting him to do something. Jane's legs were now spread wide apart, her body moving to the exact rhythm of his thrusts. The sheets had been kicked off. She moaned with pleasure, intermittently licking his chin, wanting . . . wanting all of him. Then, just as Martin started to come, as Jane dug her fingernails into his back, the ground shook beneath them.

There was breaking glass and falling plaster and the shattering noise of an explosion. Jane's eyes opened wide and she looked up at Martin, transported out of her pleasure. 'Wow!'

'It wasn't just me.'

They disentangled, flew out of bed, opened the shades and looked out of the cracked window. Fire and smoke poured out from the floor beneath them.

'It was my room,' he said.

'. . . So, I'm sorry if I'm late.' Martin stood before Drysdale wearing the same clothes which he had worn to dinner the previous evening. He had just explained about his rude awakening. Hotel employees had managed to extinguish the fires caused by the bomb under his bed before firemen arrived. But all he had been able to salvage from his gutted room was a toothbrush which now stuck out of the breast pocket of his ocean-blue cotton shirt.

'I told you you need our protection.'

'Were you protecting me a couple of hours ago?'

Drysdale only wished that he could give him the straight answer to that. 'Listen, Martin, for a man who has become an urban guerrilla leader in the Dominican Republic you seem to be a little out of touch. Don't you realize what's happening? The ELD just stormed the police headquarters. They cut off the electrical power supply to the city last night.'

'I noticed that the elevators weren't working.'

'Don't you think that we have better things to worry about than you? We'll have to move you out of that hotel. We can put you here, if necessary.' They were in an airy spacious apartment near the seafront which the CIA used as a safe house. 'I don't imagine you've got too much luggage,' he added sardonically.

At that moment the telephone buzzed on the secure line which connected the safe house directly with the Embassy.

'Where is the Ambassador? . . . Figures . . .' was all he said, and hung up. 'There's a mob hurling Molotov cocktails at the Embassy,' he said to Martin.

Tall, silver-haired Ambassador Armstrong had just fixed two glasses of champagne with orange juice in the kitchenette of his pleasant *pied-à-terre* in the Buena Vista Hotel Apartments near the yacht port. He came back to the bed, passing one of the drinks to his young mistress, Rosita. She was sitting up, stretching her slender silky arms as the satin sheets slipped off her luscious bosom. 'Have one, *mi amor*.' He gave her a gentle kiss.

A renowned deep-sea fishing enthusiast, the Ambassador routinely spent his weekends on board the yacht of his millionaire Dominican friend, Jeronimo Santobar. Just as routinely, he used his expected absence from the Chancery to sneak into his secret hideaway, and into the arms of his loving Rosita.

His wife, a Philadelphia society heiress, spent much of her time away from Santo Domingo. She did not care for the tropical heat, preferring to display herself as the Honourable Mrs Armstrong at Georgetown dinners and Virginia hunt balls. That was just fine with the Ambassador.

At the moment in which his lips locked with Rosita's for the third or fourth time and her small smooth hand started feeling into his silk robe for what she knew would be growing underneath, the telephone rang. Only very few knew to reach him here in an emergency. 'Damn.' He leaned over to pick it up.

At that moment, just outside the service entrance to the Buena Vista Apartments, five men in white overalls emerged from a van with the markings of an electricity company repair unit. The sole member of the Ambassador's special security team guarding the entrance told them to go through the main lobby to check in their IDs. A half-second burst from a silenced Heckler & Koch sub-machine-gun cut him down. Five men raced up the stairwell.

The Ambassador, now alerted to the storming of the police headquarters and the developing siege around the Embassy, was searching for his jockey shorts, which had to be somewhere around. He was going to manage the crisis from the CIA safe house where Drysdale now was. As he slipped his legs into the elastic, bullets sliced through the lock of the apartment door. He hit the floor, Rosita screamed and the door was kicked open. Three men in white overalls brandishing sub-machine-guns instantly appeared. Two had been left guarding the stairwell. The larger man with the dark expressionless face pointed his weapon down at the Ambassador, who was still on the floor. 'You are now a prisoner of the Ejercito de Liberacion Dominicano. Get your pants on and come with us.'

'Let's also take his *puta* and have some fun,' said another.

Rosita cried hysterically.

'Those are not our orders,' replied the team leader. 'Tie her up with the sheets and lock her in the closet.'

The Ambassador trembled as he reached for his boating trousers on the chair. Rosita moaned as the second man took the chance to fondle her breasts while stuffing a piece of cloth in her mouth and tying a satin sheet around her legs and arms.

There was the sound of gunfire on the stairwell. Silencers were off. One of the terrorist team who had been left on watch shouted down the corridor. 'They've blocked our escape route. There are more of them than we thought.'

The team leader pulled a hand-grenade from his overalls, and tossed it to one of the other men. 'Throw this down the stairs and tell whoever survives that the next one will explode under the Ambassador's crotch if anyone tries to set foot on this floor. We will hold our hostage right here.'

Maximiliano Perez sat alone in his tenth-floor office suite overlooking Beachside Boulevard, Miami. A brass plaque in front of the door which gave on to the carpeted corridor read: Trans Caribbean Investments Inc. He was not a workaholic and would not normally be found there on a Sunday. But today there were matters to attend.

As the main contact man for one of Latin America's most powerful drug cartels, he laundered on average between two and three billion dollars' worth of proceeds from illegal narcotics sales in the United States a year. He was also in charge of such matters as supervising bribes or subsidies to governments and terrorist organizations which were in league with the interests he represented. He devised such clever schemes as turning profits from drugs into purchases of high-powered armaments just off factory shelves – not the Soviet military surplus stuff which the Cubans usually provided – to strengthen those groups which facilitated the flow of his life blood between South America and the United States.

It was his job to remain continuously in touch and informed about everything that could affect the smooth functioning of the multibillion dollar underworld of which he was an integral part. In this capacity he had been in frequent touch with *Comandante Nueve* in Santo Domingo over the past several days, the ELD being among those revolutionaries with whom he often exchanged favors along with the M-19 in Colombia, the Chinchoneros in Honduras, Sendero Luminoso in Peru and others.

He had been given a few hours' advance warning of *Comandante Nueve*'s plans to shake the earth in the Dominican Republic and for that he was grateful. It had allowed him the necessary time to dispatch to Santo Domingo a few trusted men to protect those businessmen, politicians, police and government officials who served his interests well but who he knew were also on the ELD hit list. Playing both sides of a conflict, Perez recognized, was the only sure way of controlling the outcome.

Among those for whom Perez had ordered protection was the head of police intelligence in Santo Domingo, Major Otero, a man who had consistently helped to turn a blind eye to drug-trafficking activities and who, Perez hoped, would some day succeed Colonel Ventura as Chief of Police. Protecting Otero would also serve the purpose of allowing his men to question the Major closely about this Clark kidnapping which was so upsetting *Comandante Nueve*. That his people seemed implicated because the Arguelles home was being used as a safe house was seriously beginning to disturb Perez. He certainly didn't wish to have the ELD as enemies should *Comandante Nueve*'s revolution succeed.

He had failed so far to shed any real light on the incident, Perez had to admit to himself. Despite the equivalent of an all-points bulletin issued on this man Weinstein, throughout his network, there was little more information except a close physical description and, yes, that he smoked a pipe. Minutes earlier he had received a call to the effect that such a man had been sighted in Panama the day before, having lunch alongside a certain banker whom Perez also used. But it would stretch the limits of friendship to ask the banker about the identity or activities of other private clients. Such things were only done in cases of extreme urgency and Perez was not sure this one warranted such high priority, at least not yet.

Otero had to know something, of that Perez was convinced. When he had spoken to him before on the phone, the Major had seemed circumspect. A heart-to-heart talk would render more results. And the situation in the Dominican Republic today should lend itself to a lot of heart-to-heart talking. He expected to be getting a call soon.

Perez curled the tip of his black moustache as he looked out on to the crowded marina below his window. It was a breezy, clear day; a perfect one for sailing. He was planning to have lunch on his own forty-foot cruiser. He could use his satellite phone from there. But the trouble with satellite communications is that they could be easily intercepted. For all he knew, Weinstein was with the CIA.

The phone on his desk rang and he picked it up, there were no secretaries today. 'Max Perez . . . *Gracias*.'

They had gotten to Otero in time to keep him away from the police headquarters which was now in ELD hands. The Major had talked. It was his impression that Weinstein was with the same company as the man who had been kidnapped by FART, the Sanitex Equipment Corporation of New York.

Perez picked up the phone again, to call a friend in New York.

'The situation is really quite grave, Mr President.' The National Security Advisor was delivering his briefing

184

on that morning's events in Santo Domingo. The Presidential helicopter had landed on the White House lawn only minutes ago, flying the President back, earlier than expected, from his usual weekend at Camp David. He was still wearing his check flannel shirt with a tweed jacket thrown on top. Other members of the National Security Council gathered in the Oval Office for the hastily convened session.

'Dominican army troops arrived after demonstrators had forced their way through the Embassy gates, burning cars and killing one of our Marine guards. They could only be dispersed with gunfire. There were many casualties. We are having to evacuate the Embassy because the ELD is now holding the police headquarters nearby and bombarding our compound with mortars. Heavy fighting is being reported in various parts of the capital and perhaps most seriously of all from our perspective, Ambassador Armstrong is being held hostage under rather . . . compromising circumstances.'

'Would you care to elaborate on the last part, Mr Chief Advisor?'

The Marine Brigadier, who had recently been appointed to the post of Presidential Coordinator for National Security, cleared his throat. 'They took the Ambassador while he was in an apartment in which he keeps his mistress. His security team managed to block the terrorists' escape. It's believed that they intended to kidnap him, but now they are holding him inside the apartment and the girl is with him. She is nineteen years old, sir.'

'Nineteen years old?' The President glanced over at the Secretary of State, who was visibly upset. He had been a friend of Percival Armstrong since Yale. He had recommended him personally for the Ambassadorship. 'We have to get him out of there,' mumbled the ex-economics professor, passing a hand over his shiny head.

'I think that the only thing we can do is use force, Mr President.' It was the Secretary of Defense speaking. 'What they are demanding from us and the Dominican government in exchange for the Ambassador's life is totally unacceptable: fifty million dollars, the resignations of President Camuñas and all of his cabinet, and withdrawal of our diplomatic personnel. We've got to stick to our policy of not negotiating with terrorists.'

'What are my military options?' The President turned to look again at the National Security Advisor.

'Delta Force can be deployed to Santo Domingo within five hours. We would also mobilize the 82nd Airborne Division for a wider intervention if necessary. Our aircraft carrier battle group in the Caribbean can reach the Dominican Republic in a day with a Marine amphibious assault brigade for further backup.'

'If there is any hint of military intervention, the Ambassador is sure to die,' the Secretary of State said. 'The terrorists holding him are a suicide team, armed with state-of-the-art sub-machine-guns and grenades. They have threatened to explode one under Armstrong if they see any sign that we are going to take the apartment by force.'

'From a diplomatic perspective, I'm not sure that it is a good idea to risk a military intervention.' The Ambassador to the United Nations was just in from New York. 'Not after our invasion of Grenada. We might have gotten away with it there. But the revolution in the Dominican Republic appears to have genuine popular support. A repeat of Lyndon Johnson's Marine-landing twenty years ago would be bound to upset our Latin neighbors. I'm not sure that we could get a resolution supporting it through the Organization of American States. It could also seriously upset the summit meeting you have planned in Moscow for next month.'

'We cannot allow this hostage crisis to drag out, Mr President.' It was the Secretary of Defense again. 'Can you imagine what's going to happen when the media start pouring into Santo Domingo and we have pictures of the Ambassador and his teenage broad standing naked on the balcony with Kalashnikovs pointed at their heads. It's going to be a three-ring circus.' He turned an angry glance on the UN Ambassador. 'And popular support, my ass! Cuba and Nicaragua are training and arming those guerrillas with Soviet arms. We have highly reliable intelligence to this effect. It's imperative that you take immediate action, Mr President.'

'Sacrificing the lives of Percy Armstrong and a nineteen-year-old girl as well as inviting international condemnation.' The President spoke half to himself in a somber tone of voice.

'There might be an alternative, Mr President.' The Director of the CIA now spoke up for the first time, having arrived at the meeting late.

'And what's that, Director Hasey?'

'I have highly confidential information that a very substantial sum of untraceable money is being paid out today in the form of ransom insurance to secure the release of John Clark III, an American business executive who was kidnapped in the Dominican Republic, ostensibly by a group called FART.'

'Could I have the name of that group again, Director? I don't think that my hearing aid is working very well today.'

'FART, Mr President. In Spanish the initials stand for the Armed Workers' Revolutionary Front. The acronym does not mean the same thing in Spanish.'

'Please continue, Director Hasey.'

'One of our top men has informed me that this kidnapping is apparently a fraud.'

'A fraudulent kidnapping? I've never heard of such a thing.' The President leaned back in his chair. 'And how does that have any bearing on what we are discussing here? I don't believe that there is anything fraudulent about this group which is holding Ambassador Armstrong hostage, the ELD.'

'Well, that's sort of my point, Mr President. We know that this kidnapping of John Clark is basically an inside job by someone in the Sanitex Equipment Corporation, the company of the hostage. FART is only a front. The bulk of the ransom, which is over twenty million dollars, is going into the secret bank account which this person in Sanitex has opened up in Panama using various false names and dummy companies. My idea is to seize the fraudulently collected insurance and use it to strike a deal with the ELD to get the Ambassador out.'

'Are you suggesting that we pay a ransom to terrorists?' It was the Secretary of Defense again.

'We wouldn't exactly be paying the ransom, Mr Secretary, the ransom has been paid already, by the insurance company, all we would be doing is diverting it to the ELD instead of letting it go to FART. We would not be negotiating with public funds or anything that would appear in a corporate profit and loss statement but with an untraceable tax-exempt insurance account. Once it's been paid out, it ceases to have any official existence.'

'You aren't suggesting that we become parties to an insurance fraud, Director Hasey?' the President said.

'We can find a way of paying it back,' the Secretary of the Treasury said. 'I know the Chairman of Lloyds.'

Silence hung over the Oval Office as the President got up from behind the oak desk, turning his back on the rest of his advisors. He walked a few paces to contemplate the view of the Rose Garden through the large French window. He wore cowboy boots under his corduroy slacks. After a few moments, he turned around and faced the meeting again, looking squarely at the CIA Director.

'Assuming that we were to go ahead with this scheme of yours, Director Hasey, how sure is it that you can make the right connections to secure this ransom and talk to whoever makes the decisions in the ELD, within a limited period of time, say a day?'

'We are working on it, Mr President.'

'You've got twenty-four hours.' The President now looked at the four-star admiral who was Chairman of the Joint Chiefs of Staff. 'In the meantime, start preparations for a counter-terrorist rescue mission and a full-scale military intervention in the Dominican Republic if necessary.'

Fighting still raged in the vicinity of the bombed-out police headquarters. Despite an army counter-attack using armored cars and almost the entire air force of nine helicopters, the ELD defenders continued to resist tenaciously. One of the choppers had been damaged by gunfire and it had staggered back to its base, leaving a long trail of smoke behind it. Two smouldering half-tracks also lay disabled by anti-tank rockets. Mortars and a ·105 field howitzer had now been brought up to pound the building. The four helicopters continuing to hover overhead were dropping grenades and strafing the barracks with their mounted ·50-caliber machine guns. They were not equipped with rockets. It was slow going. The army could not spare sufficient reinforcements. The siege was already diverting enough troop strength away from containing outbreaks of guerrilla activity multiplying elsewhere around the capital. Entire slum districts which ringed the city were now under effective ELD control. The army's single tank battalion, consisting of fifteen American-built antiques, had come under heavy fire while making its way in by the airport road. The highway was being cleared, but the tanks probably would not arrive to dislodge the police head-quarters for several more hours. Previous Dominican governments had taken the precaution of stationing the tank unit forty miles outside the city to discourage coups. But such past astuteness was playing against the current régime's chances for survival.

Steven Drysdale was cramped inside a communications van which the US Military Assistance Group had set up as a mobile command post. He was being fully briefed along with his Station Chief, Mike Webb, on the grim insurgency evolving around the capital, by Lieutenant Colonel Dobbs, the permanent American Military Advisor in Santo Domingo. He had donned his combat fatigues to help direct Dominican soldiers conducting the siege. Retaking the police headquarters was top priority, Dobbs explained. From there the ELD could directly threaten the Embassy.

Drysdale had other priorities. He had just come from speaking with the cutout to his source inside the ELD. The man who had sold him the lottery tickets the previous day told Drysdale that he seriously doubted if the ELD informant would be able to conduct clandestine meetings under the current conditions. Drysdale told him to try again as the CIA was prepared to offer the ELD a deal.

The new instructions had been received from Washington just over an hour ago. Drysdale was to try by all available means to open channels of communications with the ELD through which to negotiate the secret ransom to obtain Ambassador Armstrong's release. Any incentives or 'assets' at the disposal of the CIA station were to be utilized to secure the ELD's cooperation. This inevitably meant cashing in on their knowledge of FART and the Clark kidnapping to gain favor with *Comandante Nueve*. It could ultimately mean handing over and sacrificing the group.

The specific use which had now been found for

FART was rather different from what Drysdale originally had in mind, and now he was pessimistic about how much influence FART and the real story behind the kidnapping would have in swaying *Comandante Nueve* at this point. Things were too far gone. The guerrilla insurrection seemed to be succeeding and the fanatical revolutionary leader would be unlikely to want to trade his prize hostage for a mere twenty million dollars in some underhanded deal. He would probably just think that FART had been a CIA front to start with.

The briefing was now finished. Dobbs strapped on his combat helmet as he squeezed out of the van to supervise the emplacement of the howitzer. Drysdale checked his watch.

It was time to pick up the one-and-a-half-million dollar ransom in cash which the insurance people had been instructed to deliver. Martin had tried to lie about the location of the drop but Drysdale already knew, although he was now uncertain about what to do with FART's portion of the ransom.

He emerged from the van. The crackling of automatic rifles and machine guns was incessant in the background. Soldiers with their rifles at the ready stood behind doorways as Lieutenant Colonel Dobbs got into the jeep which had pulled in the howitzer. Drysdale instinctively crouched, covering his ears as he felt the loud whizzing beat and whirlwind of a chopper coming in at roof-level for another go at the guerrillas entrenched in the police headquarters. Both towers which had stuck out of the building were now destroyed by the shelling. The only thing he could see coming out of there was black smoke. He walked briskly back to his car, keeping close to the walls of houses.

Passing the shot-out remains of an official car, Drysdale thought that at least there was one problem less to worry about. The vehicle had been ambushed that morning on its approach to the police head-quarters. When soldiers regained control of the inter-section, they had removed the bullet-riddled bodies of a chauffeur, two bodyguards and Colonel Ventura.

Tiffany Clark lay with her head on Julio's muscular chest as he switched TV channels with the remote control. In the days immediately following the news of John's kidnapping, Tiffany had tried to play the bereaved wife, staying at home in constant telephone contact with John's parents and with Lopwitz whom she hated to even speak to. She had also tried to cool things with Julio, again, as a way to redeem her guilt feelings. But after he turned up on her doorstep that weekend, her act melted just as she did. They were now back in Julio's king-sized bed in his high-ceilinged apartment on Central Park West and she could feel only steamy satisfaction. Satisfaction and relief to be away from what she knew was soon going to stop being her home.

Julio had plugged in the bedroom extension to his telephone after unplugging himself from Tiffany's last run of heat. It now rang. He picked it up from the night table.

'Yes ... *Hola*, Max ... Yes, I think that I can help you ... *Un momento*.' He held the line and turned over to look at Tiffany, squeezing her bottom gently. 'Hey, baby, who calls the shots in that company of your husband's?'

She answered him in a sleepy voice with her eyes half closed. 'The Chairman of the Board had a stroke a week ago and the guy running it now is this big fat asshole called Herb Lopwitz.'

Julio spoke back into the phone. 'Lopwitz ... he is *gordo* like you say ... *Un momento*.' He squeezed Tiffany, again. 'Does he smoke a pipe?'

'Yes, all the fucking time!' She turned over, tossing a pillow over her head.

'*Si*,' Julio said into the receiver. He hung up and reached beside the bed to pick up a copy of the Manhattan telephone directory.

Lopwitz drank down his champagne in the den of his Fifth Avenue apartment. Dick Stewart was with him. Elaine, the dark-haired airline stewardess whom Lopwitz had gotten to know on one of his many flights, filled the champagne glass, a long shapely leg sticking out of her turquoise robe. Stewart accepted the drink and thanked her, unbuttoning his blue blazer. 'Do you want some more, Herb?' She held up the bottle of Dom Perignon, looking at him across the room.

'No thanks, Elaine, I've got heartburn.'

'I'll be back in the bedroom if you need me.' She popped out of the door, closing it behind her.

'Sorry this can't be a more festive occasion.' Stewart sipped his glass.

Lopwitz lit a pipe. The news was on. Images of a bare-chested Ambassador Armstrong being paraded along the balcony of an apartment, holding his hands behind his head, as a hooded terrorist cradling a submachine-gun stood up, now flashed on the television screen. There was a glimpse of a naked girl being brought out as the image switched over to the blonde woman reporter starting her commentary at the scene.

'This may be the most serious incident yet in the crisis which has erupted today in the Dominican Republic and possibly a tragic one for a dedicated and hard-working American Ambassador. This is Jane Winter for *NBN Evening News* in Santo Domingo.'

'As you can see, our priorities have changed, Herb.'

'You mean your priorities have changed.'

'If you hand over those twenty million dollars to us,

we will make sure that this whole scam of yours remains covered up and you will face no prosecution, you've got our word.'

'I had your word this morning. Besides, I don't have the money.' Lopwitz knew that his lawyer in Panama would have switched the accounts by now.

'Don't bullshit me, Herb. Where is it?'

'I don't know, maybe the insurance people are trying something funny.'

'Herb, we may be able to negotiate the ELD down from twenty million. If so, you get to keep the difference, is that a deal?'

'The money isn't in my account, Dick.' Lopwitz puffed at his pipe. 'Anyway, I think you guys are being rather optimistic about your chances of getting the ELD to release the Ambassador for that amount. They've got you by the balls and they are going to squeeze you for everything they can get. It's going to be for a lot more than twenty million bucks, of that you can be sure.' The telephone rang.

'Herb Lopwitz here . . . Who? . . . Oh, so you are a friend of Tiffany Clark? So what kind of interests do you represent exactly? That sounds interesting. Look, come over right now, you've got my address, I assume . . . There is someone else here you might want to speak to.'

Steven Drysdale sat inside his car, watching the entrance gate into the sixteenth-century Spanish seaside fortress. One hand held a walkie-talkie, while the other clutched the Uzi that lay beside him. Despite his certainty that this was the location for the drop of the one and a half million dollars cash, there was no sign of Martin.

Three other armed men ordered by Drysdale had taken up hidden positions inside the ruins well ahead of time to guard against any possible intrusions. Despite Ventura's death, it was still very likely that other members of the police force knew about the drop and would try to take the money for themselves. The police had ceased to function as a cohesive unit since that morning and in view of the general breakdown everywhere, it was impossible to tell at this point what orders were being given and, moreover, which ones were being followed.

His security men near the tower where the money was going to be left had just communicated to Drysdale that the coast was clear. But Martin's absence puzzled him. It was just possible that he had gotten scared and decided not to turn up. Drysdale couldn't really blame Martin as the money was no longer going to go to him.

The street that ran in front of the fortress was mostly deserted. Drysdale only observed one man reading the newspaper by the bus stop near the corner. It failed to dawn on him that the buses had stopped running that day. The historic section of Santo Domingo had been largely spared from the fighting. It was lucky that Martin had arranged for the drop here. Dusk was starting to settle in. Smoke from the fires and artillery bombardments which were raging around Santo Domingo filtered the twilight through a brown haze.

The car Drysdale had been expecting now pulled up to the gate. He spoke into his walkie-talkie: 'Arrival, repeat, arrival. On standby, heads down.' A balding blond man whom Drysdale recognized as Tom Cross emerged from the vehicle loaded with two black briefcases. Another man, whom he did not recognize, followed him out carrying the other. They disappeared into the archway and Drysdale waited for what seemed like an eternity for his men posted near the tower to come back on the receiver: 'Dropping as planned, repeat, dropping as planned.' Drysdale switched on his speaker: 'I read you, over.' He had been too distracted to observe that the man reading the newspaper on the corner was no longer there, and no bus had passed by.

'Subject's exiting' was the next message on the walkie-talkie. In a few moments Drysdale watched Tom Cross and the other man emerge back out of the archway, get into their car and drive off. The brief-cases containing the money would now be at the bottom of a twenty-foot pit dug underneath the tower. It had been used by the notorious Dominican dictator Rafael Trujillo as a place to keep his political enemies. It was directly accessible from a small narrow opening on a grassy walkway behind the parapeted fortress walls. A hand-operated dumbwaiter which had been used to feed the prisoners was still in a usable state and would have just been passed down with the three briefcases.

As Drysdale prepared to get out of the car to join the rest of his team at the tower, a jeep pulled into the front of the entrance gate with five men. One of them held a rifle. The others appeared to be holding pistols or revolvers. He immediately picked up his walkie-talkie.

'There is interference, repeat, there is interference, five armed suspects . . .'

The one with the rifle who had stayed behind to guard the jeep while the others rushed inside noticed Drysdale.

Cocking his Uzi, Drysdale saw the man take aim, just managing to open the sidedoor and roll out of the car before two rounds from the M-1 shattered the windscreen. Lying on the road, Drysdale let out a long burst from his sub-machine-gun, forcing his assailant to duck for cover. He dashed across the street. When he got to the opposite sidewalk another round from the M-1 barely missed him, but he now had a clear line of fire for another burst from his Uzi which sliced the man across the waist. He replaced the spent magazine with another clip, carefully approaching the archway, past the body by the jeep. His finger brushed the trigger as he looked inside. One of the other men lay sprawled on the stone steps which led up to the parapets. Just above the body, Drysdale could make out the half silhouette of one of his security men, crouched with his Uzi.

'Don't shoot. I'm Drysdale.'

'We got him while he was trying to get out; the others are up there,' came the reply. 'We checked the IDs on one of them. They are police.'

Drysdale rushed up the steps, kicking the corpse out of the way. 'You'd better watch the entrance, make sure that there are no others.' The security man ran down.

His two other men greeted him on the grass walkway, as did the sight of two other bullet-riddled bodies. 'Where is the fifth?' They pointed towards the tower. He walked over and looked down through the narrow slit. In the darkness, it was just possible to see the glistening of wet blood on the corpse that lay at the bottom of the pit.

'Let's get the money out,' he ordered. As they pulled up the dumbwaiter with its heavy chain, Drysdale was relieved to see the three black briefcases coming into view. They were laid down on the grass. He snapped them open. They were empty.

Outside the back entrance to the cathedral, only a few blocks from the seaside fortress, Martin was getting into the back seat of a waiting cab with two brown briefcases. Martin bid a heartfelt farewell to Father Barrera, the friend of Carlos who had already saved them once. Barrera was keeping the third briefcase, filled with the half-million dollars of Carlos's share. Only half an hour earlier, the priest had signed a receipt for the delivery from Brian Thorpe, in the way which a ransom handover of this type was normally handled as Martin knew from his extensive study of terrorist kidnappings.

The couple necking at the bench on the *malecón* yesterday, where Tom Cross had picked up the instructions for the drop, had been planted there by Martin. The envelope which had been put inside the trash can was badly sealed, deliberately, to make it look as if the glue had worn off. It contained the false instructions for dropping the money at the old fortress. When Graciela and her boyfriend noticed the plainclothes man who had been following Martin opening the message as he pretended to be throwing some paper away, they had moved on to the bench. While the boyfriend hurled insults at Tom Cross for disturbing the good moment with his girl, he had slipped him the envelope containing the real instructions which Graciela had hidden in her panties.

Martin made his way to the cathedral that afternoon while Drysdale stood watch at the old fortress. He had talked with Barrera in the privacy of the priest's lodgings across the courtyard from the church.

The priest should contact Drysdale in three hours, giving Martin sufficient time to get away. He gave Barrera the unlisted phone number of the CIA safe house.

'But how can you involve me and Carlos with the CIA over a matter like this?' Barrera asked.

'The only way you are going to get Carlos and the rest of FART out of the Plantacion de Arguelles alive after Clark gets released is with the CIA's help.' Martin drank red wine from a cup which the priest had poured for him. 'Otherwise the police are going to kill all of them. The ELD wants to kill them too. If you don't believe me, you can call up Carlos and ask him right now. *Comandante Nueve* sent a dozen of his men to storm the house last night, that's why those police bodyguards are up there. And the only ones who can disarm them are the CIA.'

'But why should the CIA want to help?'

'Because they are interested in using FART for their own reasons ... it's the only way that you are going to save their lives, Padre ... attach certain conditions to guarantee their safety. Tell Drysdale that you will be representing FART's interests. If any harm comes to them at the hands of the CIA you will expose the whole affair. Go up to the Arguelles house with Drysdale and keep Carlos's share of the ransom hidden until you know that they are safely out.' Martin was pretty certain that Barrera was an honest priest. But, just in case, he emptied about one hundred thousand dollars from his two briefcases, as a donation to Barrera's personal charity.

The final exchange with the priest took place in an underground tunnel beneath the cathedral, near a treasure-trove containing some of the original gold, pearls, and rubies which Spain's Queen Isabella had given to Christopher Columbus.

The taxi wound its way through the historical streets of old Santo Domingo down to a harbor not far from the cathedral where a pleasure cruiser was lifting anchor for Rio de Janeiro in an hour. Martin was going to be on it with his one million dollars.

As he caught sight of the white ocean liner and the quarter moon reflected on the calm, still bay, he thought back to his previous night with Jane Winter. He had told her everything, except where the real drop was going to be.

14

Commander Ron Tucker peered through his binoculars over the horizon. His destroyer had been on a regular patrol off Cuban waters when orders were received the previous day to change course immediately for the Dominican Republic. Having refueled less than forty-eight hours earlier at the US Naval base of Guantanamo, the USS Wayne had covered a good distance during the night. The clear weather conditions had allowed it to cut through the calm waters at top speed in a southwestern direction.

On the approach to Dominican waters, a signal which had shown up consistently on the warship's radar, since heading away from Cuba, began concerning Commander Tucker. He had ordered a slight lowering of the speed and a twenty-degree variation in course to get a closer inspection of an unidentified vessel. His binoculars had just focused on the silhouette of what looked like a small- to medium-sized freighter in the far distance.

The communications officer, Lieutenant Buckley, walked onto the bridge from the radio cabin, crisply saluting Commander Tucker. 'We have managed to intercept messages from the unidentified vessel, sir. It is communicating in a military code of the type used by Cuba. We are able to ascertain that it lifted anchor from the Cuban naval base of Cienfuegos. We cannot clarify the objective of its mission.'

The Commander dropped his binoculars for an

instant, looking briefly at the younger officer. Cienfuegos, he knew, was a highly sensitive Cuban naval installation where the Soviets had, at one time, attempted to instal facilities for nuclear submarines. It had almost triggered another missile crisis during the Nixon presidency. 'Any results on that satellite check?' The Commander had a deep Southern drawl.

'We reported the vessel's position just under an hour ago, a satellite pick-up should be getting cleared through the CIA central computer right about now.'

Tucker readjusted the eagle-crested peaked cap back over his head. His executive officer now hurried onto the bridge carrying a computer printout. 'We have a positive identification of the vessel, sir, it's a freighter under Panamanian registry with records of participation in narcotics smuggling into the US as well as gun-running operations to pro-Communist insurgent forces in several Central American and Caribbean countries.' The Commander read the sheet. He had been briefed at a recent Caribbean Command meeting in Key West that Cuba was allowing certain protection and facilities to drug smugglers such as refueling and radar cover for their vessels *en route* to dropping-points off Florida. The same boats were carrying armaments to guerrillas backed by Castro on their return runs to South America.

'What's its course now?' The Commander lifted the visor of his cap as he peered out again through the binoculars.

'South-south-west, on a parallel course with ours, sir.'

'That's straight towards Dominican waters.' Tucker turned back to his radio officer. 'Inform Caribbean Command that we've spotted a ship on possible arms delivery to insurgents in the Dominican Republic.

Give location and ship ID. Request advisable action.'

The tall grass undulated under the wind force of rotating horizontal propellers as the helicopter with US army markings landed on the clearing in front of Plantacion de Arguelles. Steven Drysdale leaped out followed by two of his security men dressed in civilian clothes, all clutching Uzis. Four similarly armed but uniformed members of the elite counter-terrorist Delta Force had hit the ground from the chopper before it touched down. They had been detached along with the helicopter from a larger team which arrived during the night on board a C-141 Transport from Fort Bragg, Georgia, landing only hours earlier at the airport of Santo Domingo which remained securely in government hands.

The four commandos fanned out in front of the house with the twin objectives of protecting the helicopter and covering Drysdale as he immediately moved with his men to disarm three tired-looking bodyguards who had gathered on the front porch to observe the spectacle. They handed over their weapons without argument. It was explained that one was still in the back of the house and two others were posted with the Land Rover at the intersection. The shirtless man who appeared to be in charge offered to call them all in by walkie-talkie.

The bloodless coup accomplished, Drysdale gestured at one of his men who waited near the helicopter, its propeller blades now slowing to stop. A priest then emerged. He moved briskly towards the house, closely escorted by the man with the Uzi.

A perplexed-looking Carlos greeted them at the destroyed entrance, the doors still unhinged and bullet-riddled from the abortive raid two nights ago. He had just woken up and only wore his undershorts. *Cinco* huddled into his back, covering herself up with a shirt. *Tres* now also came to the doorway, with his shotgun. As one of his men instinctively moved towards *Tres*, Drysdale blocked his path, politely asking Carlos if they could all come inside. Carlos, whose expression changed to one of friendly recognition upon seeing his friend Father Barrera, said 'Yes.'

Leaving two of his men outside, Drysdale proceeded into the battle-scarred living-room with the priest, Carlos and the rest of FART, who were now all assembled, murmuring amongst themselves. He could see the shattered windows and shot-out furniture stained with dry blood. Bullet holes pockmarked the walls. '*Que pasa aqui?*' All eyes turned upwards as Nora descended the stairway, her voluptuous body covered only by a camouflage shirt.

The priest made a sign of the cross over his abdomen as the security man standing next to Drysdale let out a long whistle, then asked in a hushed tone, 'Who is *that?*'

'It's the girl they've had here taking care of John Clark.'

'Can I get taken hostage by these guys?'

Carlos went over to Nora and started leading her back up the stairs, telling her that everything was all right. Drysdale called in one of the two men he had left outside, a dark-looking Cuban American, who could easily pass for a Latin terrorist. The Delta Force commandos were now taking the grenade launcher from the men who had just gotten off the Land Rover.

Drysdale told his man, 'Get up there and stand guard outside Clark's room, don't let him out until we are ready to move him from here and speak only in Spanish, get it?' The security man gladly complied, eagerly bounding up the stairs behind Nora.

After Carlos came back down, having put on some

clothes, he went into one of the back rooms with the priest. They talked alone for nearly an hour. Drysdale sat on the living-room's broken couch, getting to know the rest of FART. *Cinco* served them warm Cokes. The electricity was still out, so the refrigerator didn't work, she explained.

When the priest came back in, he walked over to Drysdale and whispered something in his ear. The CIA operative seemed relaxed for the first time as he went in to talk with Carlos.

Following another three-quarters of an hour, Drysdale emerged with Carlos. They both wore smiles. Drysdale looked pensively around the living-room, 'Okay, Carlos, when the television crew gets here, they will probably want to do the filming over there. Get the furniture out of the way, set up a table and a chair and put up the banner with your acronym on the wall behind where you are going to sit to read out your statement. One of your guys can hood himself and stand beside you for effect. We can let him hold one of our Uzis . . .'

There had been new instructions from Washington.

Lopwitz was getting out of the taxi at the entrance to the Hotel Lima. He had caught a special flight out of New York that morning to come and take personal charge of the safe return of John Clark, whose release was expected imminently. The ransom negotiators had been instructed to fetch the released hostages at a location close to the resort hotel of La Romana. They were waiting inside the Lima now to be debriefed by Lopwitz.

The cab driver gratefully accepted the five-dollar tip before driving off.

Lopwitz dismissed the bellboy. He only carried one small bag and a briefcase. The drive into Santo Domingo had been without incident. The airport road was now secured by government troops. The occasional crackling of gunfire could still be heard coming from the direction of the shantytowns. But the fighting had died down, although certain sections of the city remained under the armed control of guerrillas and the US ambassador was still being held hostage.

As Lopwitz began mounting the steps to the front entrance, a black sedan screeched up into the empty space left by the departing taxi. Three hooded men leaped out brandishing sub-machine-guns. One of them fired a burst into the air as a warning to onlookers to stay out of the way while the other two grabbed Lopwitz and threw him into the back seat of the car. In a split second they were all inside. The one on the front passenger seat continued to fire into the air as the black sedan disappeared into Santo Domingo's afternoon traffic.

15

John Clark III just managed the backhand thrust which cast the ball over the net, finalizing the third and last set at six–love. His usual tennis partner, the Marques de Santa Ana, congratulated him warmly on the sidelines, insisting on a rematch the next day. It was November but the Mediterranean sun radiated the warm golden glow of summer. Clark had come to this European jet-set resort straddling the straits of Gibraltar less than half a year ago, along with his new wife. Their first child had been born here. He often thought of going back to America. But the pleasant tranquility of life on Spain's riviera consistently led him to postpone such plans.

His second marriage, which after only a few weeks had come under serious strain, before Clark decided to sell his family's company, was blooming here. The child unified it in love. But the relief and peace of being away from his problems in New York helped crucially.

John Clark had come home to a hero's welcome following his Dominican ordeal. An Air Force band had struck up the Washington Post march as he disembarked together with Ambassador Armstrong at Virginia's Dulles airport. The US Vice President was there to greet them along with family relations and friends. The only notable absence was that of his wife, Tiffany, who had written a note ready to be delivered to him agreeing that divorce was the best possible solution. Clark already had his mind well made up.

On their drive from the airport to his father's

Middleburg estate, the septuagenarian John Clark Jr. had announced the news that the son of which he was now so proud would become the new Chairman of the Board of the Sanitex Equipment Corporation. It had been at the personal recommendation of Herbert Lopwitz, the last thing, apparently, which the General Counsel had spoken to his father about before leaving on his ill-fated mission to Santo Domingo. It was Herbert's devotion and loyalty to the Sanitex company which was the reason why 'we are missing him today', his father had sorrowfully proclaimed during the otherwise celebratory dinner welcoming John Clark III home.

But no sooner had he sat behind the Chairman's desk, than strange things started happening. He began to receive anonymous messages threatening to expose scandalous personal information about him, about the reasons for his divorce and about the past of his stunning new wife. The company's performance continued to flag and when he failed to renegotiate an important defense contract, Clark could no longer hold off an offer from the Trans-Oceanic Finance Company of the Cayman Islands: they would cover the corporate deficit with twenty-two million dollars in exchange for a controlling share in Sanitex.

His father urged him to hold on. But his wife, his gorgeous, beautiful new wife, who made him feel like no woman ever had before and was just pregnant with their baby, begged him to sell and get away. The lawyer, who was caring for the ten percent interest that still belonged to Lopwitz, was also in favor of liquidating the shares as the money could go towards raising a ransom for the General Counsel. Lopwitz had not been insured.

His fate remained uncertain. The imponderable nagged away at John Clark even now, as he threw his tennis racket into the back seat of the Jaguar, sinking into the plush leather interior and starting the smooth ride out of the Puente Romano tennis club. He turned on the highway to cover the mile to the Marbella Beach Club where he was joining his wife for lunch.

The same terrorist group which kidnapped him had claimed the abduction of Lopwitz, at first, although no specific ransom demands had ever been made. The leader of FART, *Commandante* Carlos, made the announcement in a televised statement. But shortly thereafter FART had called for an end to armed violence, joining the ELD and other guerrilla organizations there, in a common front for peace negotiations with the government. Only a radical splinter faction, the Lucha Armada Intransigente Democratica (LAID) vowed to carry on the fight. According to the latest reports, this faction continued to hold Lopwitz hidden somewhere in the mountainous interior.

John Clark slowly passed the flower-scented gardens, covered by vines of red bougainvillea, which flanked the driveway down to the beach club, reaching a small gravel clearing at the end. He parked the Jaguar and walked through a cluster of pine trees as a view of the blue Mediterranean opened before him. Down the stone steps and across the bridge over the pool with an artificial waterfall, another sight of natural beauty lay before his eyes, stretched out topless on an orange deckchair. She flashed a radiant smile.

The group of Japanese investors just down from Tokyo studied the blueprints for the proposed luxury resort hotel, nodding their approval in unison. They were seated around a glass table on the seaside villa's spacious back porch. White-crested waves broke on the protective coral reef beyond the beach, settling the sea beneath them into a calm lagoon.

The delicately featured oriental girl, wrapped in a silk sarong, passed around the table refreshing their glasses of iced tea flavored with mint leaves. The sweet scent of Jamaican Rum tobacco wafted over the group. The rotund, cherubic-faced host, sporting a fresh growth of beard, leaned back into the canvass-covered cushions of his chair, dropping a Zippo lighter back into the breast pocket of his shirt. Shortly after his arrival in Bali, less than a year ago, he had bought up one hundred thousand square meters of prize beachside land. He was now about to triple his investment. Puffing at his pipe, he thought back to the last deal he made.

After changing cars about a mile from the hotel his 'kidnappers' drove him around a circuitous route to the outskirts of Santo Domingo. There, he changed into a Mercedes which took him the final stretch, to a dirt airstrip near an isolated beach, about an hour from the city. A twin-engine Cessna stood refueled and waiting to fly him to the next destination. A group of men unloaded the last bags of what looked like a white powdery substance from the plane to place in another aircraft which was on the runway.

It was midnight when Lopwitz arrived perspiring and exhausted from his long journey to the interior air-conditioned conference room of the Bank of Panama. No provision had been made for him to shower and change clothes. Important discussions were already in progress.

Dick Stewart, who sat across the conference table from *Comandante Nueve*, was getting visibly impatient with the revolutionary leader's unbending attitude. Lopwitz quietly took a seat next to his Panamanian attorney, *Señor* Miranda.

'You better face it, *Comandante*, you're through.' Stewart slapped the table, unbuttoning his shirt collar with the other hand. 'Your revolution is over. The Plan Zero is a zero.'

'We still have the Ambassador,' *Nueve* replied.

'If you hadn't taken the Ambassador, our navy may not have been alerted and those arms that Castro was sending you would not right now be in the gunsights of one of our destroyers.'

A look of resignation crept over the *Comandante*'s stolid demeanor. *Comandante Ocho*, who sat beside him, looked away in embarrassed silence.

Julio, whose drug bosses had arranged the eleventh-hour conference, sat at the end of the table, also in silence.

Stewart continued, 'If our terms are not met, the President of the United States is informing the Dominican Government of our sighting and the moment that ship enters territorial waters, the USS Wayne will have authorization to seize it with the arms. When your links between Cuba and the drug bosses are fully exposed, your patrons aren't going to be too pleased.' Stewart cast a brief glance at Julio. 'Do you honestly think that Cuba is going to send you more arms any time soon after that? The Soviets have been leaning on them to cool down support for leftist insurgencies as part of Gorbachev's new foreign policy. Furthermore, the seized cargo from that ship will give us the perfect justification to intervene militarily in the Dominican Republic. We are already stepping up our military aid.'

Comandante Ocho whispered something in *Nueve*'s ear, nodding his head.

'If this meeting is not concluded to our satisfaction by sunup, *Comandante*, that will be it. We are boarding that ship and our Delta team which is already in Santo Domingo will take that apartment in which you have the Ambassador, even if it kills him and the girl. As bad as it might make us look, you are going to seem even worse getting kicked by us while FART' – Stewart looked towards Lopwitz – 'continues holding hostage the Chairman of a New York corporation.'

Comandante Nueve almost said something, but *Ocho* stopped him.

'You are going to be running out of ammunition pretty soon, *Comandante*. Repeat our terms, Steve.'

The CIA Deputy Station Chief in Santo Domingo, sitting next to Stewart, now spoke. 'After the order to release Ambassador Armstrong and his girlfriend, Arturo Cayetano will resign as *Comandante Nueve* of the ELD which will then merge in a joint front with the FART under the leadership of *Comandante* Carlos. Through the appointed signature of Father Barrera,' Drysdale turned briefly to look at the priest on his left, 'a charitable foundation will be set up here, financed by the Trans-Oceanic Finance Company now being formed in the Cayman Islands. When said company liquidates the assets of the Sanitex Equipment Corporation, one third of the proceeds will be channeled through the charity to promote projects for the Dominican poor and to fund political activities by the new guerrilla coalition towards negotiating fair elections and a just peace in the Dominican Republic. The other two-thirds . . .' Stewart cut him off, gesticulating with his hand.

Lopwitz lit his pipe. The price for Sanitex, once controlled by Trans-Oceanic, had already been set with Julio's people. They would pay two hundred million dollars. From his share, Lopwitz had to pay back the insurance company, with interest, but that still left him with forty-five million. It was half of what he had originally expected to get from the deal. But under the circumstances . . .

'For the good of the Revolution, *Comandante*,' it was *Comandante Ocho* speaking, 'you must agree to the terms.'

'Here is the telephone number to Ambassador Armstrong's apartment.' Drysdale passed a slip of paper across the table to *Nueve*. 'It's working . . . we guarantee you and the men holding the Ambassador safe passage out of the country.'

Comandante Nueve picked up the phone.

Lopwitz looked forward to a night's rest as he entered his suite. She was in there, waiting. He handed her the passport with a visa for the United States. 'You keep John Clark happy, hear. Make sure that he goes on doing everything you ask.'

He stretched out on the bed.

Nora licked her lips.

A NOTE ON THE AUTHOR

Martin Charles is an American writer living in Europe. Born in Manila in 1955, he has worked as a counter-terrorism analyst and now freelances as a journalist. His assignments have taken him to Central America and to the Gulf war which he covered for American and British newspapers.